W9-BYZ-028

prince of lost places

also by kathy hepinstall

The House of Gentle Men

The Absence of Nectar

kathy hepinstall

prince of lost places

G. P. Putnam's Sons New York

This is a work of fiction. Names, characters, places, and incidents either are the product of the author's imagination or are used fictitiously, and any resemblance to actual persons, living or dead, business establishments, events, or locales is entirely coincidental.

G. P. Putnam's Sons
Publishers Since 1838
a member of
Penguin Putnam Inc.
375 Hudson Street
New York, NY 10014

Published simultaneously in Canada

Library of Congress Cataloging-in-Publication Data

Hepinstall, Kathy.
Prince of lost places / Kathy Hepinstall.
p. cm.
ISBN 0-399-14936-8
1. Mothers and sons—Fiction. I. Title.
PS3558.E577 P74 2002 2002024825
813'.54—dc21

Printed in the United States of America
10 9 8 7 6 5 4 3 2 1

This book is printed on acid-free paper. ♾

To Grace Peddy Cooley,

writer,

beloved aunt,

and friend of literature

acknowledgments

Thanks to Maria Massie, Alexis Hurley, Jeremy Ellis, Robert Keane, John Evans, J. Michael Kenny, Kathy Patrick, Terry Brooks, Judine Brooks, Anna Jardine, Lionel Bourge, Stacy Creamer, and Phyllis Grann. Thanks to all the reps at Putnam, especially my friends Mary Ann Buehler, Michael McGroder, Raylan Davis, and Jon Mooney. Thanks also to Aimee Taub, whose brilliant editing greatly improved this novel.

Polly Hepinstall, Becky Hilliker, Anne Young, Liz Erickson, and Robyn Komachi read early drafts, and I appreciate their comments and support.

Lee Wilson was once very kind to a lady in a bookstore. Thank you, Lee, for moments like that.

prince of lost places

After I am gone, you will study my life for the answer to what I did. You will talk to my neighbors and read my unopened mail. You're wasting your time. Ask the children instead. If I could, I would have taken every child with me.

I have no regrets.

one

The detective hated it when people looked at his face. A sideways glance, and then another, longer one, directed at the scar. Reddish pink, in the shape of a leaf. He'd had a fight in a bar one night, dead drunk, and someone had stabbed him in the cheek. Usually he wore a beard to cover the scar, though every now and then he'd shave it off, hoping that people's glances had returned to normal. Yet here was another man, in the open doorway, shaken by grief and worry but still allowing himself a curious stare before he turned his eyes away.

"You're the detective?" the man asked.

"Yes."

"I'm David Warden."

The man in the doorway was dark-haired and handsome, and had a few days' worth of stubble on his face. The detective shook his hand and followed him into the living room. The man did not ask him to take a seat, but instead slowed his steps and moved to the side. The detective was used to people acting like this, deferring to him, as though he could ascertain the whereabouts of a loved one from the angle of the venetian blinds, the imperfections in the wainscoting, the color of a lampshade. He obliged the man, moving about the room, looking at the fireplace and the deep-blue sofas, the chintz curtains that hung motionless over the window. A single painting covered half the wall above the mantel. It showed a vast coastline, a churning ocean, a glob of sun up in one corner that had spilled a drop of yellow into the blue sea, leaving a dollop of green. In the far distance of the picture he could see the tiny figure of a horse and rider.

"Martha bought that," the man said, "at one of those starving-artist sales. She'd sit here in the mornings, drink her tea and look at it. I don't care for it much myself."

The detective nodded, put his hands in his pants pockets and said nothing. His fingertips touched an old wrapper at the bottom of his pocket.

The man turned and led him into the kitchen, where the sink was piled high with dishes, mail spilled from the tabletop, and the answering machine blinked with a steady red purr. "Sorry for the mess," he said. "I'm not much for the bachelor life."

The detective shrugged in response, but his eyes took in everything even as he heard the irony and slight twang of anger in the word "bachelor." The mess in the kitchen of a true bachelor had the feel of permanence, and if dishes were piled in the sink, they had an inherent stability, like statues or trees. But here, pots were still on the stove, stacked on top of one another, sending out the aroma of dried chili. This man probably kept his office neat as a pin. But to restore order to the room his wife once dominated would be the first step in acceptance; this man was far from that state of mind.

The detective followed him through the dining room, around to the mahogany staircase, and up to the second floor. The man stopped in front of the bedroom at the end of the hallway.

"This is my son's room."

"Duncan?"

"Yes."

The window shade was up, and sunlight fell on the fabric of the twin bed against the far wall. It was a typical boy's room, an assortment of stuffed animals and posters and computer games. Puzzle boxes were stacked on an orange plastic desk; an action figure, posed on the top box, brandished an orange scepter.

The detective opened the door of the closet and studied the contents. "Did she pack his clothes?"

"Some of them. And a few of his toys. I don't know if she took any of his soldiers. He had so many." The man opened a drawer and pulled out a handful of little green figures. "There," he said, as though they were proof of something. "There, there." Suddenly he threw them against the wall. They fell to the ground in their various poses.

The detective said nothing.

"She's sick," the man said. "Her mind has left her. She's in no condition to be wandering around somewhere." He picked up the soldiers and put them back in the drawer.

They went across the hallway to the master bedroom, which was large and sparely decorated: some rosewood furniture, a couple of table lamps, and a flokati rug. The detective toed the edge of it as the man sat down on the bed.

"I can't believe they're gone," he said, his voice faltering. "I mean, one minute everyone's here. And then you wake up one morning and . . . that's it. It makes you wonder about God. Do you believe in God, Detective?"

The detective shrugged, walked over to a nightstand, and picked up a framed picture. "When was this taken?" he asked.

"Three months ago."

He looked at the picture and saw another version of the man before him. The smile was quiet and confident. The hair neatly combed, the tie straight. The woman next to him was pretty and small. She had her face turned at a three-quarter angle; her eyes shone. Nothing in her expression suggested a plan to abandon ship, leave the house empty, turn into nothing, vanish. And the boy. His body listing slightly. His hands flying out at odd angles. An open mouth, caught in the middle of some screeching remark designed to foil the shutter at the moment of perfection. Two seconds after this picture was taken, he was off his mother's lap and on the other side of the room, bounding toward something more interesting. The detective remembered taking his own son for family pictures, years before. To boys, portraits were slivers of church. Boring, with a reverence directed at something unseen.

The detective set the picture back down. "I'm going to need to look through your wife's papers . . . any letters, diaries. Any old prescriptions. Canceled checks. Credit cards. I'll need the phone records for the last month or two. I need to know where she worked. Her habits. I need to talk to her friends. I need to get a complete description of the vehicle, tires, taillight pattern, bumper stickers, all that."

The man nodded but he seemed resentful, as though he'd let a stranger take hold of his chin and study his watery eyes. "You used to be a cop?" he said.

The detective stiffened. Maybe David Warden knew a bit about his story. Maybe he was trying to even the score a little. Loss for loss.

"Yes, I was. A few years ago."

"Why'd you become a detective?"

He didn't answer.

"I hear you're good at what you do. The best. I hear you have amazing insight into people. That you're a chameleon when you're on a case."

"Maybe. But I never turned a color my ex-wife could appreciate."

The man didn't smile. "I'm not just hiring you to find her. You need to bring her back. I don't care how much it costs. I don't care what you have to do. I'm hiring you because I heard you're the best."

The detective thought of the woman in the picture, and the boy. Between them they had such vitality. No wonder the house seemed dark without them.

"She's very fragile," said the man. "She was a good mother. Still is, the way she sees it. I love her. You ever love someone who's crazy?"

The man was trembling. His words were too fast and running together. His gaze seemed unfocused.

"I don't know if I've ever loved someone who's crazy," the detective said at last. "When I'm in love, I guess I'm pretty crazy myself."

two

I thought I'd feel different, watching that old station wagon burn. My husband, David, had bought it secondhand six years ago, after we had Duncan. That car was good to us, and I could never have imagined that I'd be standing next to my boy in the middle of the desert, watching the flames, under starlight so strong I could see the seats blackening. I suppose that as a wife I felt a little guilty, but as a mother I felt exhilarated. I had soaked some newspapers in gasoline and put them in the front seat and lit them, as my child watched from a safe distance away. Then I ran, huffing and puffing, unsure of the progress flames would make through the car, or if the whole thing would go off like a bomb and lift me high above the cholla cactus and the prickly pear. When I reached Duncan the fire was burning bright. He stood motionless. I thought he was going to ask me what I was doing, but he didn't. He was probably the only person left in the world who still trusted me. I sat down cross-legged on the cool desert ground, pulled him onto my lap, and together we watched the fire move through the car. When the gas tank blew, the station wagon raised its back end as though bucking in a rodeo full of sensible family cars, and Duncan let out a single loud cry that contained no fear—more of a war cry, really—and I knew he had never been so proud of me. I had destroyed something so big, and in such a big way. His father could have taken him to a million baseball games and never achieved the same effect. I could feel his heart beating fast through my body, the wind blew the scent of gasoline on us, and right behind it the sweet aroma of creosote flowers. I always thought the word *creosote* meant something that came from a chimney. Apparently, though, it is also the name of a desert shrub. The old man, my co-conspirator, once told me that out here in the desert, creosote hangs in the air after a summer rain. If I ever were to cross his path again, I would tell him that an act of arson could release that same fragrance.

As the fire lost its power, ashes began floating out of the wreckage, circling over our heads and dropping down upon us. My clothes turned black here and there, and when I rubbed my face I crushed more ashes against my skin.

Back in Ohio, they thought I was crazy. Doctors and neighbors and even my husband, who at that moment was no doubt in the midst of some scheme to track me down.

But the tales of my madness were lies. I was utterly sane.

. . .

Centuries ago, the Rio Grande was strong and wild; it fought limestone on its way to the sea, and then sank down tame enough for our rubber raft. This was our second day on the river. My son lounged on the other side of the raft, facing me as I paddled. In the canyon walls around me, I saw the decorations of a peaceful spring: blooming rock nettle and ocotillo, and mud nests full of baby cliff swallows. Most of the flowers were unfamiliar to me, and although I used to run a flower shop, there were few parallel species I could think of in Ohio. Duncan was humming a song. I couldn't quite make out the melody, something he'd learned from a jingle on TV, or a Tejano tune he'd picked up from the car radio as we drove through Texas in the night.

We entered a narrow gulf between two high canyons, and a blanket of shadow briefly fell over the raft before the river turned a corner and we floated out into the sunlight. The shallow rapids carried us from one shore to the other, bumping us against Texas and then Mexico. "Isn't it amazing, Duncan?" I said. "Two totally different countries, all within a few yards of each other."

"I want to get out!" he begged. "I want to go to Mexico!"

"No, honey, we won't be able to stop for a while."

He sadly eyed the foreign shore not five yards away. I stretched out my bare foot and nudged his knee.

"You're not bored, are you?" I said. "I mean, you should be sitting in school right now. Learning fractions or maybe how to spell, or painting a cow or something. That would be really boring, huh? But you're special. You get to ride down a river with your mommy. How many boys your age get to do that?"

"None. But Tommy's father has a farm."

"I hear the farm is in foreclosure."

"What?"

"Nothing. You're having fun, though, right?"

"Yes, Mommy." His dimples were so pronounced that they made me feel even guiltier. I had lied to my son. Not a little white lie but one as vast as these canyons. But the color was coming back to his face, a bit. He had looked so pale back in Ohio.

"I'm worried about him," I had told David a few days after the tragedy.

"I'm worried about you," he'd said. "Very, very worried."

"What if he's wounded, David? Traumatized for life? How can I help him after what he's seen?" I was trying to wash the dishes as I spoke. My hands were shaking. I felt something stab me, and when I lifted my hands out of the water, I saw that one of my knuckles was bleeding. My husband came up behind me, caught my arm, and held it high as blood ran down.

"It's all right," he whispered in my ear as he guided me to the bathroom. "Stay calm. Stay rational."

This was my calm. This was my rational. I had abandoned David and his advice, turned instead to a river and its course into the middle of nowhere.

"Mommy!" my son now exclaimed, and I followed his pointing finger. The head of a tiny swallow appeared in the round opening of a mud nest. "It's a baby bird!" Duncan tried to get to his feet.

"Sit down, honey! That's a swallow. Did you know that giant birds used to fly over this river, and their wings were big enough to stretch over our pool back home?"

Duncan's eyes turned glassy. He covered his face.

"The big birds are gone now, honey," I said quickly. "They're fossils. Fossils can't hurt you."

I had packed carefully. I had canteens and insulated blankets. I had polypropylene rope, Ensolite pads, wool clothing, iodine tablets, dried food, moleskin, scissors, twine, a fishing pole, a deck of Old Maid playing cards, and an anaphylactic shock kit. I had a Coleman stove, a broken railroad watch, two old Hollofil sleeping bags, a hunting knife, flashlights, carbide lanterns, canned beets, Mars bars, John Denver music, matches, and Spam. I had a portable CD player that ran on batteries. I had one backpack full of nothing but long-burning candles. And I had directions down this river, whispered to me by an old man and committed to memory. For the past day and a half I had looked for landmarks. A fishing camp on the Texas side. A narrow island that split the current into two channels. The remains of a pump house, whose ladder was still attached, and missing several rungs. Petroglyphs on a dry arroyo. A sharp bend in the river. A canyon in which two boulders, shaped like the heads of cows, created a class II rapid.

"We have everything we need, son," I told Duncan confidently, my voice perhaps a bit too high, my words a bit too fast. "We have our own food, and we can always eat off the land. Juniper berries, yucca blossoms, century plant hearts."

"I want spaghetti."

"Duncan, you will finish your century plant hearts or you will get no dessert."

He stared at me.

"That's a joke," I told him.

He gave me a smile that meant my attempt at humor, not the humor itself, was amusing, then wiped the sweat off his face. Duncan was supposed to be sitting in his first-grade class right now, which was no longer held in the main building, but in an extension building made of corrugated tin, across the west side of the playground. When the teachers wrote on the blackboards, the sound echoed through the tin, and when the children were let out for recess, they had to run only ten feet to get to the monkey bars.

All across the country, first-graders were writing on tablets. Teachers were pacing the classrooms. Gym coaches were blowing their whistles. Janitors were pushing buckets of soapy water slowly down the hallways. And the smell in the buckets was vaguely that of hospitals. It trailed through to the classrooms. The children sniffed it and thought of sick days, humidifiers, and ginger ale.

And my son was a truant, drifting down the river with me.

One day last fall, when class was still held in the main building, someone from Duncan's school called me. He had fallen off the monkey bars and cut open his chin. I rushed over to get him and take him to the doctor, a man with a cheerful face whose glasses kept sliding down his nose. He put three stitches in Duncan's chin and smiled at his story. Duncan told him he had been racing three other boys to see who could reach the top of the monkey bars first. A group of children had gathered to watch. Duncan was first to reach the top. He won.

"And you fell?" asked the doctor.

"No. Not then."

He fell when he turned around to see if Linda was watching him. Linda was the girl who lived next door to us. In that doctor's office, decorated with posters of the Muppets, I imagined the scene. Duncan straining to catch a glimpse of her in his moment of triumph, his fingers slipping, knees falling through the bars, the world turning upside down and his teeth clacking as his chin hit metal. That is love, son. It has ruined many a playground.

"Was Linda watching you?" asked the doctor.

"No," said Duncan, ducking his head, the stitches giving him the look of an older, more world-weary boy. "She was watching a race on the slides."

Back on the river, my muscles were starting to ache from moving the oars all day. The water had turned calm and my son was asleep, his face pointed up at the shifting clouds, his eyelashes long and blond. I myself had barely slept, filled with the fear that my husband would catch up to us.

David's job was to look for oil. He was good at it. He could find oil in a Zen garden. Around the office in our home there were pictures of him wearing a hard hat in Algeria, standing in the rain in Dubai, meeting with the president of the Philippines. David looked regal, his hands clasped behind his back, his expression polite. He didn't care that much for niceties. People bored him, I thought. I used to stare at those pictures when he was away, imagining myself in those exotic locales.

I knew that he was no longer searching for oil, but for us and as carefully as I thought I'd covered our tracks, I was daunted by the task of eluding his pursuit. I pictured him pacing around our kitchen, speaking urgently into the phone, interrogating a neighbor or the teenage girl who helped me out at the shop. On the kitchen table were saucers and plates and pieces of paper on which he'd have written down notes, clues, and theories. I would have loved to have my husband in this raft with us, wearing madras shorts and no shoes on his feet. But his presence here required his sanity, which was gone, perhaps for good.

. . .

Duncan awoke as we passed an arroyo whose dry walls contained the giant oyster fossils I'd been told to look for, a sign that we were very close to the cave. Carrizo cane lined the river. Between the cane and the canyon walls lay a stretch of rocky land, bristling with mesquite trees. I felt a breeze against my face and remembered an old John Denver song, something about flowers, and the wisdom of children.

"John Denver was a misunderstood genius," I told my son. "Like your man, Barney."

"I hate Barney!" he shouted with sudden vehemence. Duncan was at the age when he deeply regretted loving Barney and would rather not have been reminded of the hours he once sat in front of the television, awestruck.

"Who do you love now?"

"You." He knew he'd said the right thing, the perfect mother-son thing, and he grabbed his feet and rocked back against the side of the raft, pleased with himself.

"You're good." I could feel the horrors of Ohio leaving me as the canyon walls of Texas and Mexico hovered on either side of us like protective parents, a mixed marriage that produced clean wind, tarbrush, swift water, and cinnabar.

The dangers of the desert were ancient. Flash floods, scorpions, rattlesnakes, frostbite, loose rocks, mountain lions, heat stroke, the barbs of the cactus, the sharp edges of lechuguilla. For centuries, mothers here knew what they were in for. They weren't sideswiped like the mothers in Ohio. I would teach my son to be careful. I would say, "Duncan, beware of five-sided leaves and snakes with shovel heads. Don't put your hands in strange places. Don't bother creatures that warm themselves on rocks. Drink lots of water, and don't ever sleep in a dry wash. Do you understand, son?"

And he would nod.

He was a good boy, most of the time. So timid in his crush on Linda that it broke my heart to see it. Even at six years old she favored gauzy, delicate dresses and carried around the same white shell-covered purse. She had the face of an angel, flyaway blond hair, and a way of walking that demonstrated a belief that the world could be conquered so easily; it was a vast, stupid place in love with pretty girls, and the rewards were endless. She would prowl up and down the sidewalk, pushing a carriage full of Knickerbocker dolls. On the occasions when she pushed too hard and the carriage turned over, her dainty shrieks would send Duncan racing out of the house, where he would perform doll triage as she stood by, barking orders at him. I wanted to tell my son not to fall for girls like her, that she and her dolls were trouble, that she would always be the boss and he the servant.

Duncan had a set of army men he played with on his driveway, dividing them into platoons, sending them on secret missions. They were brave men, stoic in their fixed positions, and the afternoon would fade as they advanced inch by inch down the driveway, past puddles and pine leaves and discarded toys. Linda would come out wearing her gauzy dress, to interrupt his games. She would stop the army and assign the soldiers to duties of her own choosing, which had nothing to do with battle. Once she even took a pair of fingernail scissors and cut off a soldier's arms, taking away the plastic hands and the gun they held too.

"Look what you did!" Duncan protested. "He can't fight!"

"He was tired of fighting," Linda said calmly. "He wants to dance."

I wondered why my son couldn't stand up for himself. *Put that soldier here,* Linda would say, *and that one over there. Make the soldiers guard my dolls.* Sometimes she would take an interest in one of the plastic men and slip it into her shell-covered purse and bear it back home to live, captured, on her pink desk or in the bottom of her closet. There came a time when I had to go next door and explain to Linda's mother that Duncan's battalion was so ravaged by theft that it no longer could protect its flank.

The boat bumped another boulder, startling Duncan.

"It's okay, baby. We're almost there. I packed three of your soldiers. I knew you'd want them."

He crossed his arms and cast his eyes downward.

"What's the matter, honey?"

"Nothing."

"You miss Daddy?" My heart sped up at the question.

"Not yet." He was used to his father being gone. I used to wonder if Duncan was different from other boys because his father was away so much. Maybe something about the way a father grabbed his son and roughly tickled his stomach instilled the confidence to keep his toy soldiers from being stolen by a blond-headed girl.

"I miss Linda," Duncan said. His eyes filled with tears, and I realized my mistake. The mention of his soldiers had reminded him of her, that blond-headed pretty little thief.

"Oh, honey," I said, putting down my paddle and reaching over to touch his cool face.

Linda had been dead for nearly three weeks.

three

I owned a flower shop five blocks from my house, on a promenade that included a yogurt shop, a dry-cleaning store, and a small grocery that sold tiny artichokes that looked harmless as sparrows but always stuck me when I touched them. An old man came into my shop every other week and bought fresh carnations. He lived alone. Not one but two wives had died in his arms, and now he preferred an armload of tulips, which he would take back to his home and arrange in a vase full of aspirin water. They helped him remember the strange, bubbling laughter of wife number one, or the floral housecoats of wife number two, which covered her knees but not the birthmark on the inside of her calf. If he stared long enough at the flowers he could recall certain visions: a picnic on a spring day, dry ice settling around a canister of ice cream, a pear ripening, a single drop of warm milk leaving the tip of a baby bottle and sliding down a wrist.

He had a theory that our loved ones don't die on their own; we let them die. We violate some rule. Maybe it happens when you scrape a carrot more than required and a sliver of perfect flesh falls into the sink. You just never know, he said.

Of course the old man was mad, or so I thought. Once when I rang up his order he glanced at some pink roses behind the glass door of the refrigerator and said: "I've seen pink snakes."

"Pink snakes?" I said, as bold numbers appeared on the register. "I've never heard of such a thing."

"They're coach whips," he said. "You can find them lying on the road in Texas, down next to the border. They look like candy, they're so pink."

"Texas? Did you live down there?" I asked.

"I lived near the Rio Grande, in the Chihuahuan desert, in a cave." He smoothed the crinkled paper around the tulips. He liked them with raffia. "I went down there after my second wife died."

"How long did you live there?"

"Two years."

"But why would you want to live in a cave?"

He didn't answer right away. He was retying the ribbons that held the flowers together.

"You'd be surprised, how easy it is."

"Why did you come back?"

"My wives fought constantly with each other. They were jealous."

I blinked. "I thought your wives were dead."

He smiled. "In the desert, all things are possible."

I thought about the old man all that day, trying to picture the cave and the desert. I wanted to go home and tell my husband about it. But he wasn't home. He was traveling again.

I first met David in a bookstore in Atlanta, where I was working as a cashier. I was still in college, studying philosophy and nursing, dueling majors, the dreamy and the practical. I was dating a photojournalism student named Leonard, who made his own beer and wanted to live on the eastern coast of Nicaragua someday. He was stubborn and didactic, and when he expressed his views on politics and war, I could not get a word in edgewise. He was devoted to me, though, and he'd given me a ring, not quite an engagement ring but close enough, and we'd talked about marrying on a beach.

I worked in the bookstore four nights a week, and that job, combined with a scholarship, gave me enough money to afford a small one-room apartment near the university. I loved working at the bookstore. People were always at their best when they were searching for a book, and I would watch their faces when they opened a selection and read something known only to them. That look of awe, or boredom, or studious concentration. Like meeting a stranger for the first time and deciding what you think about that stranger from his expression, or his first few words. After the last customer left, I would walk around the darkened store, looking at the rows and rows of books. So many stories hovering around me, each with its own ruling god, its own tragedies and borders and goals. Each had its own children and its own dogs; it inhabited the shelves like houses sharing cramped streets. I was in charge of locking up the store, and I would read all night and be too tired to go to classes in the morning. The life of books became the life that should be led, and all the emotions within them became those I should have had myself. I began to look at Leonard and wonder if the love I had for him was good enough, not just for me as a woman but for me as a character. And how would our story measure up to those in the books around me?

I was working my last shift before the Christmas holidays, a Thursday night. The weather had turned ugly; every time a customer came in, a gust of wind would move through the bookstore and make my hands shiver as I worked the counter. The cold air seemed to have ruined the Christmas spirit; customers flipped through books impatiently, seemingly annoyed by the breeze coming from the turning pages.

By closing time, a line had formed all the way to the wire stand full of mugs and gift baskets, and people were starting to grumble. I worked as fast as I could, but the line grew longer. An elderly woman with fluffy white hair and a rusted brooch slid a coffee table book about Georgia flowers across the counter and asked how much it was.

"There's no price tag," she said.

"It's printed on the back," I told her, turning the book over. "It's twenty-three dollars."

"Oh," she said in a disappointed voice, "that's so expensive!"

"I'm sorry," I said. "It's a coffee table book. Those are usually more expensive."

"It's such a beautiful book. I looked at every single picture in it. I used to have moonflowers, just like the picture, in my backyard."

"I'm sorry," I said helplessly. I would have bought the book for her, but I barely had enough money to afford my own Christmas presents. I wanted to tell her that I loved flowers too, especially morning glories, but the other customers were making the vague, murmuring sound that meant they resented the wait.

"Would you like another book?" I asked the woman. "There are other books on Georgia flowers that are less expensive." I glanced at the line, which now extended past the magazine stand.

She hesitated. "No, that's all right. It's really this one I wanted." Still she didn't move. She just stared at the book as though with enough concentration she could reduce the price.

"Hey!" The voice was deep and harsh. I looked up and saw a tall man with a big red wristwatch he was tapping for emphasis. I'd spied him farther down the line a moment before. "I got three kids in the car. You going to buy that book or what?"

There was a great gulping hush in the line, the noise people make when they want to look away but can't. The old woman stared up at him, blinking. I opened my mouth to speak, but a dark-haired young man had materialized next to the woman. He turned to the tall man. "That's my grandmother you're talking to," he said calmly. He looked at the woman. "I'll get this for you. Just make me a few more brownies or something, and we'll call it even."

The woman gaped at him. "Who—" she started to say, but the young man pushed the book toward me. "Go ahead," he ordered coolly. "Ring us up."

The tall man, confused, had retreated to his place in line, and the people close enough to have heard the exchange were gazing at the young man in admiration.

It took me three tries to get the cash register open. My hands were shaking, although no one had come in from the cold for the past few minutes. Finally I was able to give the young man the total, and he wrote out a check and handed the book to the woman, who shrieked when it touched her hands. "Thank you! Thank you!" she kept saying, and they both went out the door. News of the good deed was traveling down the line. People were smiling, and the new mood so excluded the tall man that he put his books down on the counter and left the store.

After we closed for the night, I found the check and read the name. David Warden. Under his name was a phone number. I was afraid that if I waited I wouldn't do it. I counted the money in the cash register, picked up the phone and listened for his voice.

I was in love. Not the same kind of love I'd felt for Leonard, comfortable and ordinary, but grand love, epic in scope, capable of stretching the relations between Capulets and Montagues to the breaking point, or riding the *Titanic* down to its grave. I spent every waking moment with David, and moved in with him the second month. Eagerly I added his everyday habits to the story of his generosity and grace. He liked to eat out of cartons and watch old John Wayne movies. After he took a shower he would dry his legs but not his feet. And instead of bringing me roses in a bouquet, he would peel off the fragrant layers of petals, put them in an empty milk carton, then set it in the refrigerator for me to discover on my own.

There was nothing I couldn't share with him. His face darkened when I told him, one night, the story of my father's death, and how I felt responsible. A week later David told me his own story, of a little brother, lost to drowning, on a family picnic when David was twelve years old. His brother wandered off the dock and no one saw him, disappearing under the water as David played football with two older cousins. And I saw in David's eyes the lifelong regret that I also felt. The never-ending question: What if we had done something different—would our loved ones still be with us? We had a common bond, two people whose failures in matters of life and death marked us, made us apologetic in a way that could never be undone.

The summer he graduated from the University of Georgia, we married, and I left with him for Houston without completing my degree. I didn't need a degree. Nursing and philosophy now folded into marriage, the only career I wanted. Looking back to those early days, I realize that he always had an air of mystery about him, a certain aloof sensibility that seemed most evident when he had just returned from a trip. But when we made love, he was mine again, so close to me that our stories shared words. And sometimes, when I opened the freezer door to get the ice-cube tray, I would find it full of rose petals, yellow and pink and red.

four

Last fall, a man walked into a store in Vermont with an AK-47 and killed eleven people. That same month, a bus blew up in Kansas. In January someone put something in a lake in Georgia that killed seventeen people who had eaten the fish from it. In early March, an unknown assailant in Florida shot an abortion doctor who was washing his hands in the sink. But now my son and I stood before the entrance of the cave, and none of this news mattered anymore.

We were several hundred yards above the river. For some reason I'd pictured this cave right on the river's edge. But then, I supposed, it wouldn't have been a secret.

I held Duncan's hand, feeling a sense of awe and power and of good work done, bringing him to a safe place over the objections of the world. At the same time I was terrified of that dark space.

"Is the cave where Daddy's going to meet us?" Duncan asked eagerly, letting go of my hand and creeping closer to the entrance, crouching down to peer inside. "Is it? Is it?"

"Yes. This is it." *And your mother, Duncan, is a liar. Daddy's not coming to meet us. That's what I told you to get you in the car without a fight.*

The old man had said that beyond the entrance lay what was called the twilight zone, where some light existed. Farther inside we would find total darkness, and creatures soft and blind, their veins running close to their translucent skin. Nothing fearful lived in those chambers, only calcite formations so delicate that they could be killed by the oils of our fingertips.

The sun was sinking fast.

"Are we going in?" asked Duncan.

"In a minute."

I'd managed to bring only part of our supplies. The rest, and the boat, lay hidden in a thicket of cane. I'd brought the candles, though, and a carbide lantern. But it looked so dark in there. My heart began to beat fast, and for the first time I worried that I lacked the courage to do this, after we'd come all this way.

Duncan was dancing. "Let's go let's go let's go!" He grabbed my hand and pulled on it.

"All right, all right!" I shook off his grasp. "I'm just worried that you'll be scared."

"I'm not scared!" he crowed. "You're scared! Mommy's scared! Mommy's scared!"

"Okay, okay. But don't blame me if some monster eats us."

His smile faded.

"I'm sorry, Duncan," I said quickly. "That was a joke. There are no monsters. Besides, we have John Denver music. Monsters hate him."

My hands and feet had turned cold, and my pulse was racing. I knew if I didn't move right then, I was never going in. Duncan would have to live in the cave by himself, and visit his mother outside every day as she cowered in the light. I lit the carbide lantern and strapped on the backpack full of candles. The entrance was so small that we had to crawl through one at a time. The cave quickly opened up to a passageway. Near the entrance there was still enough light to see, but within twenty steps we entered darkness so thick that the lantern light couldn't penetrate it more than a few feet. I smelled wet rocks and heard breathing around me. The old man had told me that caves breathed, especially before a storm, but still I had to stop for a minute and steady myself.

"What's the matter, Mommy?"

"Mommy's a little sick," I managed. The lantern lit up Duncan's blond hair and a formation next to my shoulder. Moving the lantern, I saw that the formation glowed orange and had the consistency of melted wax. "Look at that, Duncan."

His pale hand darted out to touch it. I grabbed his arm. "Duncan, what did I tell you a hundred times on the way to the cave?"

"Don't touch the statues," he said glumly.

"That's right. Be a good boy."

I released his arm and we moved on. I had never been in darkness this profound; it was heavy and smelled like old wet letters; when I breathed, it traveled down my throat. I was drowning in it, my lungs starving for the sweet, light air of an open pasture. The old man had told me that bats lived in the caves, and that they wouldn't bother us at all.

"Don't be afraid, Mommy," Duncan said, as though he'd lived in caves all his life. His tone comforted me, and I reminded myself that I had a backpack full of candles, weapons in the war against hysteria. We walked on carefully as the lantern revealed rocks and the smooth sides of the cave and occasionally a puddle of groundwater. The cave was cool but not cold. I shivered only because I realized that I had entered this place on faith alone, my only directions coming from an old man not known for keeping women alive.

We rounded a corner and the wall moved away from the light. Our voices echoed in the gloom.

"We must be in the main chamber," I said.

"What's a main chamber?"

"It's like a big room."

"Which room is my room?"

"This is your room. And my room too."

"I don't want you to be in my room! I want my own room!" Duncan stomped his feet.

"Don't be a brat. Most cave boys don't get their own rooms until they're ten years old."

He fell silent, and I saw his little fingers stretch out in the carbon light as he counted the years until he could escape his mother.

"That was a joke, Duncan. When Daddy gets here, maybe we'll find you your own room." Immediately I felt a guilty flush for using the fairy tale of David's arrival to pacify my son.

"When is he coming?"

"I told you, baby, it's going to be a while. He has to get some work done first."

"Daddy's always working."

"Yes, well. No argument there."

I set down the lantern and began lighting candles, not even pausing to see who was winning in the war of light and dark, just striking the matches and lighting the wicks one after another and setting the candles farther and farther apart.

"Mommy!" Duncan cried.

I stopped and looked around. The cave was full of light, and I was kneeling in a new world. Calcite formations were everywhere: soda straws, stalactites, stalagmites, columns, and curtains. Almost instantly their shapes suggested others: thieves, beggars, princes, tribal elders, gods, fire, giraffes, all manner of mythology and nature and religion. Three goblins pointed to a hawk, unaware of the calcite shark swimming up behind them. A witch licked at a lollipop. A lost pony ran at a gallop without losing its three-cornered hat. And a sailboat had lost half of its mast but sailed on under a sun whose rays grew over time.

A lake the size of a living room shone to my left, calcite formations rising like trees in the water. I stood up, turning around and around in the shimmering room. Once, long ago, I saw a movie in which everything in the world froze in mid-gesture, leaving the hero to stop terrible things from happening. It felt that way now, history in suspension, water dripping off the swords of pirates who might be persuaded, over millions of years, to lay their weapons down.

"It's magic, isn't it?" I said at last.

"It's beautiful," Duncan gasped. "Look at all the statues!"

"These are called stalactites and stalagmites. And these, well, these are called something else. Blobs or something. But it's all made of calcite. It's a kind of stone we don't see every day." I moved toward him and leaned down to kiss his blond head, feeling against my lips hair made even softer by this roomful of stone. My fear had left me. My pulse beat steady. I straightened up. "Let's see what's in the lake."

The water was so clear that we could see right through to the bottom, to the smooth dolomite, the darting fish. I took the flashlight from my belt and turned it on, moving the beam over the calcite trees, which glowed orange in the light. If I had gone outside I would have seen that same color, spreading out in the sky.

"Wow," said Duncan. "That's scary."

Training the flashlight beam into the water, I saw a fish moving around in a languid circle.

"Look, honey. The fish has no eyes."

"What happened to them?"

"He just grew out of them. Besides, he doesn't need them in here."

"Will we lose our eyes?"

"Not if we watch where we're going."

Duncan poked his finger in the water, but the fish seemed not to care.

"Let's go back outside, and get the rest of our things," I said, but my boy was so transfixed that I had to pull him away.

A trail of dark purple streaked the orange sky when we returned to the entrance of the cave for our supplies. It took me several trips to drag them down into the room and lay them out on a shelf of smooth dolomite that extended a dozen feet or so in all directions. In the back of the room I could see the opening of a farther chamber, black as pitch, and I wondered how far back the cave went. Maybe to Ohio. Maybe David was on the other end of it, calling. I had managed to carry the two-burner Coleman stove all the way from the river. I lit a match and held it over one of the burners as I turned the knob slowly, watching the blue flame rise.

Out of the corner of my eye I noticed Duncan over at the formation that looked like the witch eating the lollipop. He was on his tiptoes, facing away from me.

"Hey! What are you doing?"

He turned to me. "Licking the lollipop."

"Duncan! I told you not to touch anything!"

"You said not to touch. I was *licking.*"

"Same difference. Now stop it."

"It doesn't taste like a lollipop," Duncan said with a disappointed voice.

I took a package of wieners from the cooler and sniffed them suspiciously—the ice had melted our first day on the river. They seemed all right, so I put a pan on the burner and lay the wieners across the pan and listened to the sizzling sound as I opened a bag of bread. Between the food we had here and what was down in the boat, we had enough for a month or two. After that—I didn't know. I hadn't planned, although the old man had said he used to catch catfish in the river. I'd brought along some fishing line and a hook, but I didn't know what I was doing. I hadn't fished since I was a child.

"Mommy?"

"What?"

"Maybe Daddy will get lost trying to find us."

I didn't want to hold my silence too long, or my son would grow suspicious. "Don't be silly," I said at last. "Your father's good at finding things."

Duncan flopped down next to me. "I hope he brings my spaceman. I forgot to bring him."

The wieners sizzled. I turned the flame down, realizing I had to think of this room as something entirely separate from the world, separate from David. This was our new life without him. I would tell Duncan someday, when he was ready.

"Can we take pictures?" Duncan asked. "Bobby won't believe me. He'll say I'm a liar."

My heart sank. He didn't understand that this was his home now, that those kids in Ohio would grow up without him. Duncan was a smart boy, and I feared his questions.

"Don't listen to Bobby. He's always scratching. I think he has lice." Hoping to distract him, I fished around in my pocket. "Look at this." I showed him a penny. "See how dark and old it looks? Well, the dust on these stones is magic dust." I gathered some of the dust with my fingernails and sprinkled it into the palm of my hand. I placed the penny on top of the dust and rubbed my palms together. Duncan leaned forward, peering at my hands.

I stopped rubbing, licked the penny and showed it to Duncan. "See? It's shiny and new."

"How did you do that?" Duncan shrieked.

"Magic," I said. Also known as the restorative properties of dolomite. I couldn't replace a missing father with a shiny coin for long.

I didn't know how much time had passed. We could hear an owl calling from the entrance, but in the space around us, all was silent. I took off my shirt and my pants and walked barefoot over the smooth stones to the lake, my naked son following me.

I dipped my toe in the cold water, then stepped down onto a shelf, then another, until the water came up to my chest. I looked down and saw my toenails clearly.

Duncan stood shyly by the water's edge. I stretched my arms out to him. "Come here, honey."

"Is it cold?" he asked uncertainly.

"Yes. But you'll get used to it." I had a memory of Duncan standing by the edge of the pool in our backyard, crying, while David, waist-deep in water, gestured to him.

Duncan left the water's edge and flew into my arms.

"Good boy!" I cried.

"Ahh!" he said as he felt the cold water.

"It's okay," I assured him, making a slow circle in the water as I held him. "See, that's better, isn't it?"

I'd turned on the portable CD player, and John Denver music rolled toward us. A water sound, soft and sweet. Give it a thousand years and it would burrow through these walls and carve a slow path to the sea.

Duncan laughed, flailing in the clear water as I held him up. "Do you want to go under?" I asked him. It was a trick we'd practiced in our pool back home.

He nodded, and we took a deep breath and sank beneath the surface, hovering there together, in water so pure it had no taste. My son's blond hair drifted out from his face, his cheeks puffed up with precious air and his skin white as snow. I released my breath, a spray of perfect globes in the water, but Duncan hoarded his own. We rose together, bursting to the surface and into the flickering light.

The candles still burned, and wax had gathered around their bases. After tonight we would have to ration them, and sleep with just one lit. We lay down together on the sleeping bags, and

Duncan soon was fast asleep and breathing into my neck. Someday he would grow up and tell some therapist that his mother had kept him in a cave and made him listen to John Denver music. But I was unrepentant. He was safe, after all. I listened to his breath, and the older, wiser, more muted breath of the cave. White waves rolled across the ceiling, dolomite waves so vast they could brighten a million cents.

Water dripped into the lake from a calcite branch.

Calcite in its purest form made chalk.

In the other world, teachers used chalk to write numbers on the blackboard. Students copied the numbers onto their tablets. Later the janitors moved sponges across the blackboard until the numbers disappeared, but the water kept dripping. Dripping down the walls.

five

I couldn't sleep after Linda died. I put double locks on all the doors and windows, I threw away the mail, I soldered the mailbox shut, I raked my fingers through flour with sudden suspicion. How easy would it be to poison flour? How secure were the grocery stores? And the checkout people—where were they from and what were their grudges? And that horse outside, the one a child could ride on for the gift of a quarter—what if that horse had secret wires coming out of it, one red, one blue, trailing around the back of the store, to be connected by some faceless monster?

At night I looked out the window from an upstairs room and saw Linda, playing under the streetlamp, tiny winged insects swirling in the light. And when the bugs flew down, they didn't land on her but rode on the ends of her flyaway hair as she bent down to tie her shoelace. I couldn't tell David about the ghost of Linda. He didn't want to hear about her death.

"Martha," David would say, "come back to bed. You need to sleep."

"I need to check on Duncan."

"You don't."

"What if there's a fire?" I asked him one night. "What if we fall asleep and the house burns down? What if someone poisoned the bread we had with our dinner? What about diseases? I knew a woman whose son went to bed with a fever and the next morning he was dead. And meteors. Meteors strike the earth more than you think. And boa constrictors. Do you know that they escape the zoo sometimes, they live under porches and grow thirty feet long? I saw some firemen on the news last year. They were pulling one out from under a house. It was big around as a tree trunk, and it had been eating all the dogs."

"Lie down."

"One time I was washing Duncan's clothes. He'd been playing with his friend that day out at the edge of the woods. Down near the hem of his pants, the part that covered his ankle, I found two perfect tiny punctures. And they were this far apart." I showed him what I meant with my thumb and forefinger. "And my heart stopped when I held those pants up to the window and the light came through those two pinpricks, the perfect width apart that a snake would make with its fangs. I let that boy play too close to the woods. I ran and found him and pulled down his socks, and his ankles were pale and smooth. It was my fault. I let down my guard."

David got up and made me get back into bed, covering my body with his. I tried to move and his grip tightened.

"Linda's mother would never have let her play at the edge of the woods, David. Do you see the irony? She never let her daughter get on a bicycle without a helmet. And she walked to the end of the block every day and waited for the school bus. She even called the school to find out the background of the bus driver. But look what happened. Look who died."

The night before I stole David's son and vanished into nothing, I put on my robe and sat down next to him on the edge of our bed. I had seen our family doctor, and been put on a regime of different pills that were supposed to keep my pulse calm, but they hadn't been working. David had made me an appointment with a psychiatrist the next morning. It didn't matter to me; I knew I'd be leaving the next night. I'd been planning our escape for a week or two, but something David had said to me the night before made me realize I could stay no longer. I kept telling myself he'd said it in a moment of frustration and anger, that he couldn't have meant it. But deep down, I knew he did.

My husband, who thought I was crazy, was crazy himself.

In a corner of the garage, in the space behind an old refrigerator, I had stockpiled supplies and maps, and a few of Duncan's clothes were neatly folded and sitting in an overnight bag at the bottom of his closet. The air pressure was perfect in the tires of the station wagon.

David was sleeping. He has always been able to sleep at the drop of a hat. Many times, as a young man traveling the country, he would fall asleep leaning against the sides of buildings. I traced my fingers lightly against his face, stroking his chin and his nose and his eyebrows. I always found him so beautiful in sleep, more innocent, more real. I imagined how his mother had once leaned over him and loved him like this, when he was still small and the world expected only boyhood from him. I had never considered it before, this need for the perfect memory of his body and his face. I moved my hand to his chest and he opened his eyes.

"Are you all right?" he whispered.

"Yes, I'm all right."

"Did you take your pills?"

"Yes."

I wanted to tell him I had already checked on Duncan five times that night, but I knew he didn't want to hear about it; the subject seemed to drive him mad. Instead I began to unbutton his pajama top. My fingers slipped; I didn't remember the steps to lovemaking anymore. I covered my bewilderment, kissing his lips. He took my shoulders and stiffened his arms until I stopped.

"Honey?" he whispered.

"What?"

"I don't know if you're feeling up to this."

"I am feeling up to this."

"Really?"

"Really. Are you?"

He hesitated. "Of course. It's just that . . ."

"You've never had a crazy woman?"

"I didn't say that."

I began to button his pajama shirt, but realized I was going the wrong way and unbuttoned it again. He caught my wrists. "It's just that you've been so fragile lately. Maybe we should wait until after you've seen the psychiatrist."

"The psychiatrist couldn't possibly be a better lover than you."

He sighed. "Don't be funny."

"I'm sorry."

"Don't be sorry."

He kissed me, a kiss so passionate that I wanted to stop and demand that he take back the horrible, crazy thing he'd said to me, but I was afraid he would only say it again, so I kept kissing him, cautious as though creeping across a floor late at night, hoping a floorboard wouldn't squeak. I pulled off his shirt and he pulled off my nightgown and we got under the covers together, entangled in each other, but just as the lovemaking began I gave a little cry and moved out from under him, and suddenly I was sitting on the edge of the bed, my heart racing.

"What's the matter?" he asked in a bewildered voice.

"Duncan," I said. "Duncan!"

I lunged from the bed and ran naked down the hallway, into Duncan's room, throwing open the door and letting the light fall across the carpet. There he was, as I had found him earlier, asleep on his bed. He had been so tired he hadn't even pulled the covers back; he was curled on top of his quilt with his eyes closed tightly, facing the door.

I stood looking at him as David came up behind me.

"I thought I heard him cry," I said.

David sighed and went back down the hall. When I joined him in bed a few minutes later, he was lying on his back and staring at the ceiling. We lay there together in silence.

"What time is your appointment tomorrow?" he finally asked.

"Eleven o'clock."

"I'll drive you."

"No, I'll be fine."

"You don't forgive me, do you? For not being in town that day."

You're right, honey, I don't.

"David," I said, my voice neutral, "you're never in town."

In a psychiatrist's office, certain motifs are obligatory. No hard colors on the walls; those may fray already extended nerves. There will be one or two framed pictures, at most, also in soft colors, and these largely free of context: a boat on a blue river, perhaps, or a disembodied horse standing in a pasture of white space. The tables don't startle, nor do the lamps, and the track lighting is sleepy; it sifts down over the bowed heads of people reading recipes in magazines. Bottle this room, and the contents would drug a Tasmanian devil. All the same, it seethes with a peculiar tension as the occupants struggle to look nonchalant, the last defense of the truly despondent.

I regretted bringing Duncan here, who ignored the *Highlights* magazines I stacked in front of him and instead stared at a woman who sat on the couch across from us, writing something on a pad. A grocery list, no doubt, or a recounting of her husband's crimes. She was a well-kept woman in her middle forties wearing blue-framed glasses whose quirkiness I would admire in a restaurant, but here they designated loneliness, uncertainty, the inability to please a father.

"Duncan," I whispered, "don't you want to read your magazines?"

He shrugged but didn't take his eyes off the woman.

"Honey, it's not polite to stare."

The woman must have heard me, for she looked up briefly

from her list, then went back to writing. *Lettuce. Milk. Paper towels. He comes home smelling of beer.*

I picked up a *Highlights* and tried to hand it to Duncan. "Come on. Read this. There are lots of good stories in here."

He folded his arms and shook his head. I threw the magazine back on the table.

"Fine," I said. "Be that way."

The woman looked up and her eyes met mine, and I thought I detected a note of pity in her eyes, which made me bristle. After what Duncan had gone through, he was entitled to a stubborn moment now and then. The woman dropped her gaze and went back to writing, shielding her paper with one hand.

The door opened and an older man came out, bearing the unsteady look of someone who's just said more than he wanted to. The woman put down her magazine and guided him out of the waiting room.

"Aha," I mumbled to myself. "So it's the man who's nutso. She's just the driver."

"What?" said Duncan.

"Nothing."

A tall bald man in a gray suit appeared in the doorway.

"Are you Mrs. Warden?" he asked.

I nodded.

He had a kind face and smiled at me warmly. "I'm Dr. Zelmer," he said. I wondered what David had told him on the phone, and whether they were co-conspirators now, whether they talked at odd hours.

I stood up and shook the doctor's hand.

"Nice to meet you," I said. The acoustics of the room made my voice sound tinny to my own ears.

"Come on in," he said.

I glanced at Duncan, who was focusing on the doctor's striped tie. Duncan loves ties. "Dr. Zelmer, this is Duncan."

"Hello, Duncan," said the doctor.

Duncan said nothing.

"He likes your tie," I said.

"Mmmm. My wife picks them out. I'm practically color-blind."

"Come on, Duncan," I said.

He started to get up off the couch, but the doctor said, "I think I'd like to talk to you alone, at least this time."

"But I don't want my son sitting out here by himself."

He nodded. *That is exactly why you're here, Mrs. Loonybrain.* "Would you feel better if the door to the waiting room were locked? You're my last patient before lunch."

I felt ashamed, but I nodded.

The doctor's couch was a myriad of colors and didn't match the wallpaper. I sat at one end and he sat in a swivel chair across from me. His mustache was neat and his shoelaces looked new. He had a high, broad forehead and razor stubble close to his ears. All in all, he looked born to be a psychiatrist, and I imagined him in some other profession, a janitor maybe, looking for scuffs on a linoleum floor with that same patient expression.

"Your husband says you haven't been sleeping."

"I have a lot on my mind."

"He says you don't leave the house anymore. That you're suddenly afraid of the dark. And you painted your downstairs windows black."

"Yes. I used shoe polish. And I planted a cactus under each downstairs window. It's a trick I heard a long time ago. Anyone who gets through that window has to wade through a cactus first." I fidgeted with my fingers. The air-conditioning started up, making the sound of Kleenex being drawn out of a box, then shut off suddenly. In the silence I looked down at my hand, my fingers gripping the fabric armrest of the couch, and I imagined the hundreds and hundreds of hands that had come before me, sweating into the couch. Soak that armrest in a pond, and the water would turn salty as the ocean.

"Tell me about Duncan."

"I don't know where to start."

"Anywhere."

"All right. I'll start at the beginning. When I had Duncan, the doctor said there was something wrong with my pelvis. They put me under for the delivery. The doctor delivered my boy and then went home. All night long I would struggle out of sleep and say, 'Where is he?' to the nurse. The nurse would say, 'He's fine, he's fine,' and I'd fall back into some haze. When I would wake up again, I'd be afraid I had only dreamed what the nurse told me. So I'd ask about him again. By morning I was hysterical because they wouldn't bring my son to me. When they finally put him in my arms, I wouldn't give him back. I screamed at them, told them never to keep my son from me again. David was embarrassed at the way I acted."

"How did you feel about that?"

"That's the kind of man he is. He likes things moderate, usually. I've never been moderate. I'm more like my father that way."

"What do you mean?"

"He sold vitamins. And he believed in them passionately.

He didn't think there was a single thing wrong with a person that couldn't be cured by the right form and amount of some trace element. His eyes would shine when he talked about it, and I envied his faith. Believing something in your heart must make you feel so steady in this world."

The doctor leaned back in his chair.

"I don't know what will keep Duncan safe anymore, so I'm going a little overboard. Who can blame me? Can you?"

He didn't answer. I troubled him. I could tell.

"Say something, Doctor."

"So you're saying that you're fine, that your husband's over-reacting to your concerns?"

"It's not just overreacting, Dr. Zelmer. I told myself it was that at first. But something's seriously wrong with my husband. He won't talk about Linda. Linda's the girl next door. You know about that, don't you? David pretends her death never happened. And the other night he said something so crazy I think he must have lost his mind. He's been under stress, I know, but I can't believe he said such a thing to me."

"What did he say?"

"I can't repeat it. It's too awful."

"Could you whisper it, maybe?"

"I suppose I could do that." The couch creaked as I rose to my feet. I went to the doctor, leaned and said the words so softly into his ear that I wasn't sure he heard them.

"I see," he said as I sat back down. "I can understand how that would upset you." He tapped his fingers together, closed his eyes. "I think that you need to be in a hospital."

That's what David had been saying too. I had thought the doctor understood me and my need to keep Duncan safe. Now I realized that he was on David's side all along, and had betrayed me.

. . .

That night I told David the doctor was right. I did belong in a hospital. He kissed me and told me that everything would be fine, that he would help me pack my clothes. I told him I wanted to wait until morning and he said he understood. It was all so easy, lying to him.

I had already packed my clothes. They were waiting for me in a duffel bag in the garage, along with my other supplies. I waited until David was asleep and then I stole into Duncan's room. We were going on a surprise trip, I whispered in his ear. We had to go ahead of Daddy, but he would be joining us. We were going to a place where we would all live together.

Duncan rubbed his eyes. "I want to say good-bye to Daddy."

"You can't, honey," I said. "He's sleeping. Let him rest. We'll see him soon."

He believed me.

six

Duncan stood at the river's edge and peered into the depths. It was early in the morning, and cold. Goose bumps stood out on his bare legs.

"I can't see anything," he complained.

"The river's got sand and mud and stuff in it. It's not pure, like cave water."

He seemed satisfied with this answer. He straightened up and looked around, his gaze coming to rest on a cottonwood tree with low-hanging branches.

"Can we do it?" he asked.

I caught his meaning immediately. "Sure. Why not?"

The night before, he'd had his favorite dream, which I took as a good omen. Back in Ohio, he would come down to the breakfast table and report that he could fly. In his dream, he was light as a feather. He could see the tops of the trees and the chimney of our house. And from his place in the sky, our pool was the size of a piece of candy.

After drinking his orange juice, he would announce that he was going in the backyard to fly before breakfast, and I would get up from the table and follow him out to an old oak tree and watch him climb up to the lowest limb. He would crouch on the limb, his face full of such belief that a tiny part of me believed him too. He'd balance himself, his arms out at either side, and then leap for the clouds and fall into my outstretched arms with a heavy sigh, gravity scolding him, and we'd trudge back into the house, defeated.

David asked me why I kept indulging him. "Why pretend like that? He just ends up disappointed."

"I know," I answered. "So do I."

Now Duncan crouched on the unmoving limb of the cottonwood tree, balancing himself. He raised his arms and fluttered his fingers before stretching out his hands.

"Nice touch, Duncan." I took my position underneath the tree.

"I'm going to fly now," he announced. He looked down at me, annoyed. "Don't catch me. I don't need you."

"I'm just catching your shadow."

He seemed to accept this. His bare feet pushed off the branch and he plummeted straight down into my arms, his body so heavy that I almost lost my footing. I felt his breath leave him.

"I'm sorry, honey." I set him down.

He brushed off his arms as though his failure had left him dusty. "I want to try again."

"Maybe later, honey. Let's go back to the cave."

"No, no! Let's go swimming!"

He was pulling on the cuff of my shorts, when I heard a snorting sound. I looked down the river. A man on a horse was making his way toward us. I grabbed my son's hand and pulled him into a copse of carrizo cane, shushing him as we crouched together among the narrow green leaves. I didn't know if the man had seen us. I could hear the horse coming closer, the squeak of the saddle and the sound of hooves in the mud. Duncan stiffened in my arms. He'd been afraid of horses since a Shetland pony once bit him at a petting zoo.

The horse paused in front of the cane. I felt something stinging my arm and looked down. An ant. I brushed it off but felt more bites along my legs and on my shoulder. The stings were like fire, and I was frantic now, trying not to cry out as I clawed at the ants. Finally the horse gave another snort and moved away. I parted the cane and peered out cautiously. The man on the horse wore green pants and a gray shirt. I didn't know whether he was a Texas lawman or a park ranger. Either would cause me trouble. When the man and the horse disappeared around the bend, I leapt out of the cane, scratching like mad.

"Damn it," I muttered. I crushed an ant between my thumb and forefinger and turned to look for Duncan.

I gasped.

Ants covered his legs.

"Duncan!" I grabbed him and headed for the river. When we reached the muddy bank I set him down and pushed his legs into the water, my hands rubbing up and down, washing away the ants. The year before, a wasp had stung his arm, and it swelled up as big as an orange. How could I be so stupid, to let this happen in the middle of nowhere? And why hadn't the old man mentioned ants?

When all the tiny creatures had been washed off and were floating on the surface of the river, I put my arms around Duncan and pulled him out of the water.

"Does it sting, honey?" I asked anxiously.

"No."

And truly, I saw no angry red marks on his legs.

"You're okay, then?"

"Yes, Mommy. I'm okay."

I closed my eyes, let out my breath, and whispered a thank you to the drowning ants.

seven

He found it near the road that led to Santa Elena Canyon, the light declining and the clouds overhead narrowing inside a spectrum of color. He had to sit down by the side of the winding road, take out a pint bottle and drink in celebration. The burned husk of the station wagon sat on the other side of a little rise, hidden from the road save for a pair of tracks so slight he marveled at his own ability to spot them in the fading light. He screwed the lid back on the bottle and approached the car. The remains of a run-over cactus lay in the dirt, still oozing a thick sap. Most of the car was burned black, but the paint around the headlights was the beige he'd been looking for, and matched the color in the photograph he had. He smelled burned leather and other things not meant to burn. Plastic and vinyl and metals and the wrenching odor of singed rubber. She had removed the license plates, he realized with a smile. But she probably had not thought to chip out the VIN. Yes. There it was, still intact. He turned his flashlight on and read it, comparing it with the number on a piece of paper he had drawn out of his back pocket. Like reading a lottery number. You hold your breath until you get to the end.

The park rangers hadn't found this car. If they had, they would have launched an investigation and called a wrecker by now. He felt part of the secret, standing out here with the air going thin and cooling perceptibly against the sides of his face, the shadow bending out from the open door of the car. He touched the black door, wiped his hands on his pants, and went over to the rise that led to the road. He sat down, unscrewed the bottle, and took another drink.

He thought of the woman in the picture, and the blond-headed boy, the handsome man. Imagined the three of them in this car, untouched, winding through the streets of their neighborhood, among the maple trees. The father holding the wheel at ten and two, the mother gazing dreamily out the window, the son kicking the seat. Stop it, son. I said stop it, stop it. Honey, the woman says. Her pale hand reaches back, she takes the knee of her boy. Stop kicking your father.

He had to admire the woman, doing what she did. He had talked to many people about her, read her writings, followed her path. And now she seemed so familiar to him he almost didn't want to break the spell by finding her.

Born in Georgia. Lost her father young. Lived for her husband and then for her son. Loved chocolate bars and the music of Emmylou Harris. Believed in omens, stayed away from PTA. Liked to swim naked at night in her backyard pool. Carried around an old railroad watch that had belonged to her father and was her prized possession.

He took another drink. Once he had pretended for a month to be a priest. And once his good-old-boy impression had fooled a husband into showing off his mistress. This one was different. He didn't know what to become with her yet. What she would respond to.

The stars came out and the moon rose.

He'd promised himself he'd leave half the whiskey in the bottle, but when he held it up to the moon, the liquid inside turned a color that reminded him vaguely of vitamins, and so he drank the rest in the name of good health.

eight

This was the land of adaptation. The kangaroo rat, denied the right to drink, secreted its urine as a paste. The cholla cactus used its spines to shield itself from the sun. The toadhopper mimicked rocks to keep predators away. The female katydid listened with her knees, and deep inside the black cave, the fish in the lake had lost their eyes.

In this land, even a runaway mother found herself changing.

Like the eyes of the cave fish, the pills the doctor gave me no longer served a function. I poured out the contents of the prescription bottles onto a rock near the opening of the cave; the new dawn's mist made the pills melt one into another. Before the day was over, the mass had dried and worn away; a wind out of Mexico bore the calming dust north.

It took several attempts to learn how to build a fire in the cave, one that wasn't so smoky as to choke us. Within a few days I discovered the benefits of cactus flesh, the soapy properties of yucca roots, the resilience of basket grass. I worked by trial and error, having at my disposal only one guidebook and an old man's advice. I had something else, I discovered—my mother's feel for nature, a close-to-the-earth practicality I'd never before seen in myself. And I was proud. How could anyone this resourceful be judged insane?

I counted the days with pebbles; already a small pile was taking shape in the candlelight, a formation that skipped the steps required of the others and grew before our eyes. Duncan said that when his daddy came, they were going to find the other end of the cave. I nodded. I was running out of excuses, and I had no pennies left to shine.

We had come in the middle of springtime, the favorite season for those who float the Rio Grande. The flowers were beautiful, and the dangerous floods of summer had not yet arrived. Duncan played the scout. He stood on top of a boulder and scanned the distance before we climbed down to the river to bathe. In the late mornings we hid in the cane and watched the people float by. Many of them were young; they laughed and drank beer. We saw families whose children were Duncan's age; he tensed beside me as he watched them, as though gathering his courage for a dive into cold water. I sensed his loneliness, and part of me wanted to stand up and wave the children over to play with him. But instead I placed a hand on his shoulder, warning him.

"Why can't I talk to those kids?" he demanded in a whisper.

"Because we're a secret."

"I don't want to be a secret!"

"Shhhh."

Water and sun. Nighthawks, katydids, rock nettle and darkling beetle. Salt cedar and willow. Blind crayfish darting backward through the cave pool, and John Denver sputtering as the batteries began to fail him like the engine of his plane.

I set up Duncan's three soldiers around the cave. This was a peacetime mission, in a land so calm there was nothing to guard. Still, they held their guns steady as they waited, one crouching and two standing, in a forest of stalagmites.

Duncan ignored the army men. He was tired of them, and we had a new game, one we called Flashlight Stories. I moved the flashlight beam around the cave and told the tale of the formation that glowed in the yellow light.

"Once there was a little boy. You see him? See his little baseball cap?" I moved the light down. "He had a little dog. The boy and the dog went everywhere together. Of course, there was this evil witch . . ." The beam moved over to a stalactite, lumpy and wet. ". . . and the witch wanted the dog for a pet. So one day, when the boy was asleep, the witch flew over and grabbed the dog and flew away."

"Wasn't the dog too heavy for the broomstick?"

"No, it was a wind-up dog, like a Pomeranian. The little boy was terribly sad. Fortunately . . ." The flashlight beam moved again. ". . . he also had a pet wolf. See the fangs? So the boy and the wolf found the witch, and the wolf ate her and they got the dog back."

"Didn't the wolf eat the dog?"

"No. The wolf ate Barney."

Duncan had never feared the darkness of the cave; he could

move within it like the fish and the bats, knowing instinctively where to put his hands and feet. Each night I blew out two more candles, and the light receded farther and farther away. I lay next to Duncan and stroked his hair, feeling it like silk between my fingers, drawing my fingertips down to the ends, gently so as not to wake him. Our motions had been anticipated over the centuries, already turned to stone. In another chamber a mother kissed her son on the forehead, as I did with my own son. I tried hard not to think of David, but sometimes he was as real as the sticky warmth of dripping wax, and I could see not only his face but his gestures, and part of me wanted to rouse Duncan from sleep and forget all my dreams of sanctuary. Sail backward on the river, find the burned-out car and drive its black shell back to Ohio. But I couldn't. Even before he lost his mind, Duncan's father couldn't protect us any more than Linda's could protect her.

One night I dreamed that Linda was prancing around the cave in her gauzy dress, finding the stalagmite forest, stealing Duncan's army men and jamming them into her purse. She had that same queenly look on her face, that same faraway smile. When I woke up in the morning, Linda was gone and the army men were still in their place.

We were going to try fishing for the first time, an activity I'd put off for more than a week. The two of us sat on a flat rock in the river, and Duncan watched me thread the line through the eye of a silvery hook, then tie five square knots. I vaguely remembered a few fishing trips I took as a child with my mother, who loved nothing more than to put on a wide-brimmed straw hat, pull some catalpa worms off the tree in the front yard, and head for the Red River. I didn't remember much, just that I grew bored easily, and that luck, patience, and prayers could all be lumped together to make some kind of bait.

Duncan crossed his arms. He hadn't spoken in nearly ten minutes, and by the look on his face I knew a storm was coming.

"Baby," I said for the fifth time, "what's the matter?"

"Daddy's not here."

"I told you, you have to be patient."

"I am patient!" His voice rose. "I've waited and waited!"

"It hasn't been that long."

"I counted the rocks in the pile!" he shouted. "There were this many!" He flashed eight fingers. "I want us to send a map to Daddy and tell him where we are."

"Duncan, be quiet. Someone might hear you."

"I don't want to be quiet." He threw back his head and bellowed. *"Daddyyyyyyyyyyyyyy! Daddyyyyyyyyyy!"*

I caught his arm. "Stop it! Do you want to go back to the cave?"

He stopped screaming and glared at me, his face bright red. "I hate the cave."

"You do not."

"I do too."

I felt a terrible guilt, looking at him. "Why don't we do this?" I asked at last. "Why don't we draw Daddy a map when we get back to the cave tonight, and then we'll put it in an empty jar and throw it in the river."

"What if someone else finds it?"

"We'll put his name on it."

This seemed to appease Duncan somewhat. He hugged his knees and watched me tie one more knot.

"Look!" I said triumphantly, holding the line up so that the hook glinted in the light. "I tied a fishhook, Duncan! My mother would be so proud. Wait a minute. Damn! How do I put the sinker on?" I sighed and cut the line, threaded the bell-shaped sinker on, and retied the hook. "That doesn't look right either," I said, inspecting the rig. "The hook is wearing the sinker like a hat."

Duncan turned his head to gaze at the limestone cliffs of the canyon downriver, where rock nettle grew.

"Well," I said, "I guess it will work. Now we have to put on a bobber." The bobber proved to be wily as well. I pressed the top of it, and a little hook came out of the bottom. But a hook stuck out of the top too, and I wrestled with the contraption until my fingertips grew sore.

"Duncan, you're good with your hands. See if you can put the bobber on for Mommy."

"I don't want to."

The heat shimmered off the rocks. My face was sweating and my frustration was growing. "Duncan, honey, can I ask you a question? Do you see a Long John Silver's anywhere around here?"

"No."

"Then help me!"

He wasn't listening to me. The gurgling water had all his attention, or the wind in the cane.

Finally the bobber behaved, and I cut off a piece of Spam with a pocketknife and molded it onto the hook. "There's catfish in this river," I said, trying to be Duncan's friend again. "Big ones. I've never caught a catfish before, but I hear they're good to eat."

"I don't want fish. I want chocolate."

"Do you see an Easter bunny around here?"

"You're not funny."

"I've heard." I threw the bait down into the water and waited, the other end of the fishing line wrapped around my hand. The bobber sat as motionless as my son. I pulled the line back in and saw that the Spam was gone from the hook. "Must have fallen off," I observed. "I'm going to write the Spam corporation about their defective product." I cut off another piece, baited the hook, and tried again.

"Daddy always keeps chocolate Kisses in the drawer in his desk," Duncan said suddenly, accusingly. I knew. Many were the times I'd gone looking for a pen in that drawer and had to burrow through a nest of crumpled foil.

"We have other things besides chocolate. We have peppermint."

"I hate peppermint."

"Since when?"

Silence again. He had every right to hate me. I'd taken him away from chocolate and his father.

Without announcement, the bobber disappeared under the surface of the water, and the line tightened around my hand. I could feel something struggling beneath the surface.

"I've got something!" I shouted, trying to control the shaking of my fist.

Duncan looked vaguely interested. He squinted down into the water.

The muscles in my arm were beginning to ache. The bobber darted around in a tight circle just beneath the surface. Sweat poured down my face. The fish felt like a monster; the line bit deeper into my fist. At last I stood up and walked the length of the rock, dragging the monster along with me. I jumped from the rock and kept going, gritting my teeth and pulling with all my force. When I looked back, a huge catfish was flopping on the bank, its fins digging in the soft dirt, thrashing out a sand angel and then lying still, its sides heaving. The thought that it might have real lungs and a real heart, red and warm, filled me with pain.

Duncan ran down the rock, jumped to the bank, and bent down to inspect the creature. "Does it bite?"

"I don't know." Gingerly I reached down and tried to turn it over. The catfish jerked, and one of the spikes along its spine entered my hand. I cried out, pulling my hand away. The pain was searing and hot. Blood started to drip from my palm, and I was grateful for the look of concern that came to Duncan's face.

"Mommy!"

"Mommy's okay," I said calmly, tangled in fishing line and dripping blood steadily.

"Are you hurt bad?" he asked anxiously.

"No, baby. He just finned me. I didn't know fish were so dangerous."

Blood came from the catfish's mouth, and it emitted a low, plaintive moan, like a hurt cat meowing.

"He's crying!" said Duncan, forgetting all about me and my wounded hand.

"He's not crying. He's just making a funny sound. That's why they call them catfish, I guess."

But the plaintive sound continued, stabbing at my heart. The creature's eyes were pitch-black and expressionless, but its sides pumped in and out and its tail twitched.

"Mommy, throw him back! Let him live!"

A knot had formed in my stomach, and my hand was throbbing. I closed my eyes and took a few deep breaths. "Honey, I can't throw him back. He'll die anyway. See? He's bleeding. I don't want to kill him. But we have to do this. We have to eat. He's just a fish. He won't feel a thing."

The catfish cried again.

"Mommy," Duncan said decisively, "you're mean."

He followed me silently back to the cave as I climbed up the rocks, wary of cactus and nettles, my good hand holding on to the tangled line and the dangling fish. It was heavy, at least four pounds; my arm ached. I felt a drop hit my knee when I climbed over an escarpment, and the sensation made me look to the sky for a rain cloud, then down at my leg, where I saw my own blood running.

When we reached the mouth of the cave, I set the catfish down on a small flat rock. My mother used to talk about skinning catfish. I had no idea how she did it. My head pounded. I found a large, smooth stone and knelt down next to the fish. "Duncan," I said, "go into the cave and get Mommy her pocketknife."

"No."

I looked up at him. He was standing there, bare-chested, arms crossed.

"Did you say 'No' to me?" I asked, a warning in my voice.

A drop of my blood fell on the fish, whose black skin was starting to tighten in the sun. "I'm not asking you, Duncan," I said. "I'm telling you to go into the damn cave and bring me my damn knife." My voice was rising. "Does Mommy look like she's having a *good time,* Duncan? Well, I'm not. I'm doing this because this is what I have to do so we can have fish for dinner."

"I don't want fish!" Duncan screamed. "I want *chocolate*! And I want *Daddy*!"

I stood and glared at him. "'I want *chocolate.* I want *Daddy.*'"

My voice was high and whiny, mocking him, and I imagined my own contorted face, my ugliest face.

The catfish moaned behind me.

"We have only been out here for eight days. How many times have you actually seen Daddy in the past six months, Duncan?"

This seemed to take him aback. His mouth fell open. He looked at his hand. A little thumb folded over, a pointer finger. He was counting. My heart broke.

"Baby," I whispered. "Mommy's so sorry. Mommy didn't mean that."

Duncan's thumb and finger uncurled.

"Mommy just wants you to be happy. That's all. Aren't we happy here, baby?"

He didn't blink. "*You're* happy." He turned and darted away, disappearing behind a stand of trees.

I stood there, shaking. My teeth chattered. I sank to my knees beside the fish. "Do your children give you this much trouble?" I whispered.

No Flashlight Stories tonight. I got only half the skin off the fish, and when I was turning it on the spit it looked like it was wearing a fencing jacket. Duncan wouldn't eat any of it. Wouldn't talk to me at all.

After dinner I sat at the edge of the lake, washing my hand in the cold, clear water. Blood leaked out of the slit in my palm; it seemed to attract the blind fish, which swam around the pink cloud in circles. Duncan sat cross-legged on his sleeping bag, nibbling on his thumbnail and staring off into space. He was still bare-chested; the paunch of his white belly hung over his pants.

"Do you want to come swimming with me?" I asked.

He shook his head. I felt ashamed, like something dirty and oily in this beautiful cave, corrupting the water and poisoning the bats and killing the living stone. I crawled out of the lake and walked slowly over to the sleeping bags, dripping water, and lay down in my soaking-wet clothes, feeling the heat of the nearest candle against my face. Duncan lay down as well, facing away from me. I closed my eyes and smelled mesquite, blood, guano, and martyred fish.

I woke up in a panic, my heart beating wildly. I threw a hand out and felt an empty sleeping bag and the hard ground beneath it.

"Duncan," I whispered. "Duncan!"

I fumbled for the matches, couldn't find them, ran my hands through solid darkness. "Duncan!" I whispered. "Please, answer me! You're scaring Mommy!" My hand hit something that rolled away. The flashlight. I turned it on and swept it around the room. It showed me columns and knobs and figures and the sharp glass of the lake, but no son. Again I ran the flashlight around the room. Again I saw nothing. I got up and stumbled toward the opening of the cave, sweeping the light around me. When I reached the entrance, the cool desert air hit my wet clothes and I shivered. "Duncan!" I called. "Duncan!"

I could not find my boy. My bare legs brushed against lechuguilla, my bare feet scraped on rocks. I tripped and fell. My knee split open. I scrambled to my feet and broke into a run, stumbling around stones and trees. Light poured down from the full moon and the stars in the sky, but nothing moved in this landscape. Frantically I worked my way back down to the river, parting cane and shouting as loud as I could, begging Duncan to answer me, telling him I would never kill another fish, telling him I would do anything he wanted me to do, and that I was sorry, I was sorry.

Frantic, wet, cold, and bloody, I looked for him for an hour before a thought struck me hard.

Maybe he hadn't left the cave.

I turned and scrambled back up the canyon. At the opening of the cave my bare foot stepped on something hard and sticky, something that rolled underneath me so that I lost my footing and fell on my back, turning my head to find, staring three inches from me, the fish's severed dark head.

Duncan and I had been to the chamber behind the main room, but we had ventured no farther than that. I limped to the back wall of that chamber and entered the corridor that opened next to a camel with three humps. The air was thick with bat guano here; it burned my eyes. The corridor opened into another room. I turned my flashlight upward and saw a ceiling full of orange teeth. I walked around slowly, careful not to knock into a column or step on something sharp.

When I reached the center of the room I stood and listened, training the circle of light around the new formations, the new stories. A man with wings. Seven eagles fighting over a nest. Pegasus bucking off a one-legged pirate. A chess set in which the king was perpetually trapped. And in a corner, a young formation. Six years old and growing.

nine

For twelve years, my father drove all over Georgia in a two-toned Impala, selling vitamins. We didn't have a lot of money, and he had only one suit to wear on his trips: a double-breasted pinstripe, a little too big in the shoulders. He was a great salesman, or so my mother told me. He truly believed that certain vitamins could loosen joints and fortify blood and give a pink tint to the skin that meant the capillaries were alive again; he took this belief door to door with him, speaking urgently to housewives and old women and pale, thin children in whom vitamin B-12 was a stranger. He had one good pair of Windsor shoes, and my mother would polish them before every trip and leave them by the bathroom door. I sat on the edge of the bathtub and watched the ritual: He would shave carefully, comb bay rum through his hair, then put on his suit and his freshly black shoes. When he leaned down to kiss me good-bye, he would smell brisk and fresh and vaguely fruited.

Across our back fence grew a spreading carpet of morning glories, originating from a packet of seeds donated by my saint of a grandmother. At a very young age I thought that if I slipped a bloom or two inside my father's glove compartment I could afford him some divine protection on his trips. When he returned, his shoes faded, I would sneak into the garage and open the glove compartment, and the dried blooms would fall out, their mission complete. He never mentioned them to me; I don't know whether he ever noticed them or had any idea of their power.

When I turned ten, I stopped putting blooms in his glove compartment; I was busy doing other things. I'd discovered my mother's hot rollers, and I spent my time gazing at my new curls in the mirror. One day in early May, my father was hit by a drunk driver just outside Athens, Georgia; he died in a hospital two days later. I couldn't help thinking that I had failed to protect him; selfishly I had attended to my own curls. I grounded myself for months, sat in my room and looked out the window and prayed for another chance.

When Duncan awakened, his mood had improved drastically. He hummed a morning song to himself as I seethed on my sleeping bag. Brat. The wound on my hand still throbbed, the soles of my feet were tender, and a scab of dried blood covered my right knee.

"Mommy?" he whispered.

I kept my eyes closed, pretending sleep. He was just a boy, I told myself, but I couldn't help remembering my panic in the dark, and imagining how he'd stood there in the recesses of the cave and listened to me shriek his name.

I heard him rummaging around, and then silence. When I opened my eyes he was nowhere in sight.

"Duncan?"

No answer.

I put my clothes on and walked from our chamber to the opening of the cave in pitch darkness. Duncan stood with his back to the cave, looking at the rising sun, still humming his song. He stopped when he heard my footsteps.

"Isn't it a pretty day, Mommy?" he asked, turning around and smiling. "Look at the sun! It's all different colors."

"Very pretty," I said sullenly. Beetles had found the catfish head and covered it with their black bodies. Ants had found it too. A whisker and an eye were gone.

"Did you sleep good, Mommy?"

My heart melted a little. "Pretty good."

The catfish head was making me sick. I shouldn't have left it so close to the cave. I looked around for a stick with which to move it, and my eye fell on something near the entrance.

I picked it up.

"What is it?" Duncan came closer.

"It's a Hershey bar."

"Chocolate?" he asked, excited.

I let my breath out. We'd been discovered.

How quickly people clutter a space with their own things, attach themselves to it, so that moving from it hurts. I spent all day lugging our supplies through the corridor and into the farther chamber, working by flickering candlelight; it was too dark to see, really, and I floundered in the shadows.

I wouldn't let Duncan eat the chocolate bar. It wasn't safe. He didn't want to leave his room, the lake he'd grown to love. And the soldiers looked so natural at their posts in the stalactite forest, he complained when I moved them.

"They'll be happy guarding a new room," I told him.

"The ground is too bumpy here," he said. "And it smells bad."

"That's bat guano. You'll get used to it." When I spoke I heard a strange catch in my voice, and it bothered me. I'd heard that sound before. It used to come just before my heart began to race and my thoughts lost their sonar and collided with each other in a swirling cloud. I used to have medicine for this condition, but it had turned to dust, and now lay in the crease of some cowboy's hat in the Panhandle.

We were a mother and a son, vulnerable and weak, and someone from the outside world needed only a flashlight to enter ours. Whoever had left the candy bar must have heard our argument about chocolate the day before. Yet I took it not as a kind gesture, but as an act of war.

"I hate this room," Duncan said.

"You liked it enough last night," I barked at him, then immediately regretted it. His shoulders slumped.

"Oh, Duncan." I ruffled his hair. "You just scared Mommy, that's all. But I have a surprise for you. We're going to do something fun."

"What?"

"You'll see."

I picked up a cottonwood branch I had dragged into the cave earlier, and began whittling it with the pocketknife, which was still bloody from the fish. Duncan's eyes widened as he saw a weapon take shape. He wanted to play. He readied his soldiers.

Twenty minutes later I had a spear, bent slightly in the middle but so sharp I could barely press the tip with my thumb.

"I want a spear too!" Duncan shouted.

"Maybe for Christmas."

"I'm bored. I want to go outside." He moved restlessly about the cave, spinning around with his arms outstretched until he grew dizzy and fell on the ground.

"Tomorrow," I said, but I wasn't sure when we would be safe again.

Before we slept I rolled some rocks in front of the opening to the corridor, and stacked a few on top.

"How will we get out?" Duncan asked.

"We'll move the rocks back."

We lay down on our sleeping bags, my spear next to my right hand.

"Are you afraid, Mommy?"

"Of course not. Don't be silly."

I hadn't played music in a few days because the batteries in the CD player were low. But I needed John Denver tonight. Since I had to listen for any noises coming from outside this room of mud and stone, I turned down the volume until his voice was merely a whisper. His lyrics tonight didn't sound happy. They sounded like a warning. After a few minutes I turned off the music and lay awake in the dark, my eyes wide open.

The next morning I took the rocks down and cautiously ventured out of the cave. Just beyond the entrance, I found another Hershey bar.

ten

I crouched in the moonlight, spear in hand, watching the opening of the cave from behind a tree. Duncan and I had spent another day cowering in the new chamber after the discovery of the second chocolate bar, and I had decided that we would be prisoners no longer. Now, while Duncan slept, I waited for the stranger.

The crickets were out tonight, and the wind blew my hair in my face. Things were in motion around me, creatures that skittered through dead straw and in the leaves of the trees. The bluff creaked like an old house as I listened for footsteps. I heard a sigh to my left and looked quickly, catching a glimpse of something that could be a gauzy dress.

"Linda," I said, and the wind blew the gauze away from a cluster of shimmering leaves.

I could remember so clearly every part of the day that Linda died, every gesture, every word.

That morning I put a peanut butter and jelly sandwich, an apple, and a Snickers bar into Duncan's lunch box. I held Linda's hand and Duncan's too, walking between them to the bus stop. The conversation we had was merely a group of distracted words, look at that, or when did we, or what do you think. You could take those words and use them as the basic pattern for any conversation. You could propose marriage with them, or sell a painting. I put the children on the bus and went to work.

The old man came in, and he seemed more wistful than usual. He told me a story about wife number one. They'd rented a cabin and lived by a lake for two weeks, and he helped her wash her hair in the lake. He remembered how the shampoo smelled like jasmine, and how her hair felt like silk moving through his fingers. I tied his flowers and sent him on his way. And there was nothing out of the ordinary, nothing unreasonable.

At one-thirty a woman I didn't know came into the shop and stared right through the roses in the refrigerator, as though in a trance. I asked if I could help her, and she said, "Did you hear?" Of course I didn't hear. There was no radio in the shop. I was arranging flowers in a vase, and when she spelled out the news to me I stopped what I was doing and ran out the door, leaving the bouquet with too many Shasta daisies and not enough ivy.

It wasn't safe to be driving on the streets that day. Ferocious mothers were trying to get to the school, jumping curbs and speeding through traffic lights, cutting off other drivers, veering off the road and back on again, worse than drunks. The police had the school cordoned off, sirens wailed, helicopters circled overhead. The smell of cut grass and the slight scent of gunpowder. A fat policeman with a rattle in his voice kept pushing us back, waving his arms, and the group of mothers huddled together until we were really one mother, we knew the same recipes and tied the same bows, we sang lullabies in the same pitch, we had one fear and one wish. Behind us our cars had been parked haphazardly, some with the keys still in the ignition. News reporters were everywhere but no one would talk to them. I craned my neck, looking toward the school. The children were being held somewhere. No one knew anything.

Out of the corner of my eye I saw Linda's mother. She was shorter than the rest of the women, and was standing on tiptoe trying to see. Her face was strained, and a muscle that began in the arch of her foot was tightening in her neck. Later I replayed her image in my head over and over, but in my imagination I put my arms around her waist and lifted her high above the crowd of mothers, her body so small and light.

Dawn arrived in the desert. The stars were gone and the sky was pink, but the moon lingered among the clouds. My neck ached, and the spear was heavy in my hands. I heard the morning critters crawling toward rocks that would heat up by noon. I was about to go back into the cave, when I heard a footstep. Not one of the indistinct kind based purely on imagination and the natural settling of branches, but one so clear that my heart stopped. I crouched and waited.

Another footstep. I crept closer, staying low to the ground. That stranger would not go into the cave, where my son was sleeping. We would have a bloody battle first, and scientists from the future would find our remains, removing the soil with their tiny brushes until they saw my skeleton embracing that of the stranger. Through the bones of his rib cage they would find the nicked wood of my crafted spear.

I held my breath as the stranger came walking up to the entrance of the cave so casually one would think he was delivering the mail. In my hours of waiting and in my state of dread, he had grown thirty feet and darkened to the pitch-black color of a demon, taken up weapons and traded in his voice for an ominous snarl. But the pink light of morning had stolen all his horrors. The man I now saw was tall and lanky, wearing tattered, faded jeans, desert boots, and a T-shirt with a plaid shirt thrown over it. A knapsack was strapped to his back. He had a narrow, friendly face and tousled light hair, and as he knelt down he paused to scratch at a full beard. He reached into his shirt pocket and pulled out a Hershey bar, holding it up as though to shield the sun's glare with a visor of chocolate. Then he placed the Hershey bar carefully near the entrance.

I leapt out from my hiding place with a shriek. He stared up at me, frozen.

"What are you doing here?" I demanded, my spear aimed at his heart.

His mouth opened and closed. I didn't expect this stillness from him. I thought he'd be fighting me. I was ready to fight him. Destined for it, I thought.

"Whoa, sister," he said finally from his kneeling position. "No need to run a spear through my guts so early in the day."

"What do you want?"

He smiled and pointed at the Hershey bar, as though it were a letter sent with him by the elders of some foreign tribe and it would explain everything.

"Yes, I see the Hershey bar. Why did you bring it?"

He put his hands out, palms toward the hazy sky. "It was just a gift. I heard you talking about chocolate the other day. Thought you might be hungry. That's all." His beard was the rusty color of stalactites stained with trace elements of iron.

"I don't want your chocolate. You're a stranger to me. I don't know you. What do you want with us?"

"Like I said. Nothing. If I'd really wanted something, don't you think I would have gone into the cave?"

I didn't answer him. I was almost disappointed with the fact that he didn't frighten me. My adrenaline was a useless liquid here, like Windex or cologne. Suddenly I was so tired I could barely stay on my feet.

"Can I get up?" he asked.

"Yes. But don't come near me."

He stood up, stuffed his hands in his pockets, and kicked at a stone. "If you don't like Hershey bars, I've got jawbreakers."

"I'm not falling for all your candy talk." I shook my spear a little for emphasis. "I'm not afraid to use this, if I have to. You see, I've learned a lot about myself lately. I used to think I couldn't hurt a living soul. But I could, if I was cornered, if I had to. I could without blinking an eye. Maybe that makes me evil. I don't know."

He looked at me a moment and began to laugh. He laughed so long he closed his eyes and held his stomach. "Your spear," he gasped, "is crooked."

"So? It's sharp."

He made a great effort to stop himself from laughing. When the snickering had subsided, he opened his eyes, let his hand fall from his stomach, and straightened. "Throw it at me."

"You'll be sorry."

"Do it."

Still I hesitated, and as if aware that I needed one more threatening gesture to kill in cold blood, he took a step toward me. I threw the spear at him. It traveled a few feet and zinged off into a bush, scattering purple berries.

We stood there in the silence.

"Two out of three," I said.

He retrieved the spear and handed it to me. "I could make a better one for you."

"That would defeat the purpose, for some nomadic killer to help fashion weapons against him."

"I'm a nomadic killer?"

"Or just a pest. I haven't really decided."

"You're funny. What's your name?"

"I don't have a name."

"You're very mysterious. You should meet my ex-wife. As far as I'm concerned, she doesn't have a name either." He extended his hand, then let it drop when I didn't take it. "I'm Andrew. I'm sorry I scared you. I didn't mean to. I just heard your voice the other day, and you seemed scared, or angry. I'd seen you once before, bathing in the river."

"You did?"

"I didn't see anything," he said quickly. "I turned away."

"What do you want? Why are you here?"

"You mean, here?" He spread his arms wide. "In the middle of nowhere? I just want a little peace. Somewhere I can go and maybe forget about someone."

He looked forlorn. I sighed and lowered my spear but didn't ask him to explain.

"Come on," he said. "Tell me your name."

"It's Martha."

"That's a nice name. So Martha, what—"

"Listen, it's been nice talking to you and I wish you well, but this is my cave, and more importantly, my secret. I have to ask you to leave me alone. I've been through a lot, and if you really are as kind as you look, you'll respect that."

"I know you've been through a lot. A woman would have to have been, to come out to this desert and try to live by herself."

I almost reminded him that I wasn't alone, I had my son with me, but I stopped myself. "I get along fine, for a crazy woman."

"Craziness is very subjective. Especially out here. I've been accused of craziness by women. By my account, it was just love."

"Good-bye, Andrew." I threw down my spear and walked toward the cave.

"You're doing a few things wrong," he said.

I paused and turned. "Like what?"

He glanced around and noticed the catfish head. "You're not supposed to leave any kind of food around the entrance to a cave. It attracts animals and insects, and you don't want that. Also, you need to be very careful bathing in that river. It's got pollutants in it. It even has traces of cyanide, near the old quicksilver mines. Just don't let it splash in your mouth."

"How about the catfish around here? Are they safe to eat?"

He shrugged. "Never hurt me."

"How long have you been out here?"

"Don't know. I don't count the days. Why bother if you're never going back?"

I didn't know why I was still talking to him, why I hadn't sent him on his way. I realized, suddenly, how lonely I'd been. But his presence here was a threat to me. If he could find me, David could find me too.

"Why pick this desert, out of all the other deserts?" I asked him.

"I had a friend back in college who was a graduate student in geology. He was writing his dissertation on the rock formations out here. I camped out with him on the river for a month one summer. He always said this desert's magic. That here, all things are possible."

I remembered the old man's words. He had said the very same thing, and I had a quick vision of him trying to separate his angry wives as they splashed each other in the river.

"Let me explain something to you. I didn't come out to the middle of nowhere just to deal with another crazy person. According to my husband, I'm crazy enough on my own. So if you . . ." I stopped speaking. Duncan, half dressed and sleepy-eyed, stood outside the cave.

"Daddy?"

"Duncan!" I shrieked. "You get back in the cave!"

Duncan looked at Andrew. "You're not Daddy."

I went to my boy and turned to Andrew. "My son wanders the earth, looking for his daddy. You see, I'm very promiscuous and he has no idea who his daddy is." I touched Duncan's shoulder. "Duncan, this is Andrew. He was just leaving."

"Hey, kid," said Andrew. "How you doing?"

"Did you bring chocolate?" Duncan asked.

I answered for him. "No, he didn't, honey. Go back in the cave." I turned him around and gave him a push. Duncan moved a step and stopped, so I gave him another push, then another. Finally he ducked into the cave and disappeared.

"He's hardheaded," I said, turning around. "But he's a good boy, especially considering what he's been through."

"How old is he, Martha?" Andrew's voice was soft and concerned. If he was a bad man, he was truly one of the great desert actors of our time. My name sounded strange to my ears. The last person to say it was David, the night before I left. He said it in my ear, in our bed, in our house in the suburbs. Now my name sounded alien. Maybe it wasn't Martha, after all. Maybe it was Julie, or Gretchen. "Duncan is six. We want what you want. To live in peace. It's a big desert. Go someplace else."

"I understand peace. I just worry about you, that's all."

"You don't even know me."

"Are you sure you'll be all right?"

"I'm positive. I'm happier than I could ever be in the real world."

He looked at me. "I understand that. I'm happier here too. I'm getting my life back."

"Well, just get it back somewhere down the river."

He picked up his knapsack. "One more thing," he said.

"What?"

"I don't think you're crazy, any more than I am."

I watched him walk away, this stranger with my father's name.

eleven

All this time the cave had kept the bad dreams out, denying them entry along with celestial light. Now it let the nightmare take me away, put me back in Ohio, and pressed my foot down on the accelerator of the old station wagon. Up ahead I could see the school, police sirens flashing and TV crews pointing their cameras toward the red-brick building. All the mothers had gathered. All except one.

Old and sick, she was sleeping. Later the police would awaken her, because her son died at the school as she slept. She would say, It's not possible what you tell me. My son was a good man. He gave part of his checks to me every month. He fixed my plumbing and my heat. And the cinquefoil that lined my driveway is entirely due to him. He could not possibly have done this. You have the wrong man.

Now I was in the group of women who stood in the schoolyard, some of them in suits, having found out in the middle of their workday. One still clutched a pen; the mothers were packed so close together that this woman had scribbled on the pale sleeve of the woman next to her. Around me women were weeping.

Policemen and mothers never gather until it's too late. They have that in common, and their own helplessness enrages them. A policeman was approaching us, and we fell silent, Linda's mother still small, still standing next to me, still up on her toes. And the policeman seemed to be walking in molasses; time crawled as he approached us. The silence around me was complete as the crowd parted around Linda's mother, the cop walking toward her with a look on his face that I couldn't quite read. This was a terrible lottery; it could have been any of us, but we backed away from Linda's mother. We gave her a wide berth and felt relief.

At the last moment the policeman stopped. He turned his head and looked at me.

twelve

We spent the morning moving back into our original chamber, where stories still held their old forms, back to our lake and the smooth stones upon which I laid our sleeping bags. I worked silently, disturbed by my dream. Andrew, the stranger, was to blame. Harmless though he seemed to be, he took our solitude away from us. I knew that going deeper into the cave wouldn't help us. I had no more control over our fate here than I did in Ohio. My own helplessness haunted me.

"Who was the man?" my son said for the hundredth time.

"I told you, Duncan, over and over, he was a stranger. He was just passing through."

"His name is Andrew?"

"Yes."

"Why did you make me go back in the cave?"

"Because you're not supposed to talk to strangers."

"I could have given him a message. And he could have given it to Daddy."

"Andrew wasn't going that way."

"Is he coming back?"

"No."

Duncan looked disappointed. "Maybe someone else will come. Maybe a kid I can play with."

"Don't say that!" I caught myself and continued in a lower voice. "We have to be careful, honey, who we talk to. Remember, we're trying to be a secret. Right?"

"I don't like being a secret. It's boring."

Our provisions had lasted twice as long as I thought they would, but the canned meat was running low, and I decided to try fishing again, God help me. It was still early enough in the day that there wouldn't be many rafters out on the river, although we needed to be careful.

"Don't give me any grief," I told Duncan as I gathered my fishing equipment. "We're going fishing and that's that!"

"Okay, Mommy," he said cheerfully.

"You live to keep me guessing, don't you?"

"What?"

"Never mind."

When we reached the river, sunlight had already filled the center of the gorge and was spreading outward, in the same manner that people fill a movie theater. We sat down and I began to fish. Thirty minutes passed and my bobber remained motionless. The catfish were still asleep, or telling the story about their friend who went out for a bite of Spam and never came back.

"Mommy," Duncan said, "let's go to the canyon."

The canyon walls were full of cliff swallow nests, and he wanted to see the babies. Duncan had always been fascinated by birds. One day when he was four years old he found a baby bluebird at the edge of the woods. He brought it home and put it in a shoe box. The next afternoon I looked out the kitchen window and saw him kneeling next to the box in the backyard. I couldn't tell what he was doing, so I went outside to investigate. When I looked in the box, I saw that the little bird was dead. And Duncan was kneeling there with his eyes closed. I asked him what he was doing, and he opened his eyes and said he was trying to pray the bird back to life. "I'm sorry, baby," I said. "The bird's gone. You have to accept that." I put my hand in the box and lifted out the bird, its body cold and smooth. I wanted to tell him that there was nothing wrong with his prayers, that the failure wasn't his. Duncan buried his bird by a gardenia bush, and in the aroma of that bloom he kept the grave free of buttonweed an entire month.

Remembering this, I ruffled Duncan's hair. The story of the bluebird was a mother's story. It needed no beginning or ending, and its epic quality came not from great wars or great adventures, but from a cut on a finger, a grade on a paper, something wild found in the woods that didn't occupy even the space of a cupped hand. I could have told stories so brief they were only details: his hands reaching up to catch something I tossed to him, the way he bit his lip when he drew, the posture of his body in the presence of cartoons. A crayfish moving away from the flicking of his fingers, darting backward into a paper cup.

"Why are you smiling?" Duncan demanded.

Little boys would never understand the silly ways of their

mothers, how they could one minute scold them and the next love them so much they might come apart.

"I'm smiling because I'm happy. And yes, if we're very careful not to be seen, we can fish in the canyon for a little while."

I sat on a low rock and watched my bobber swirl in an eddy. It was hard to tell sometimes whether what I felt was current or fish, the pull of water or a living thing. Duncan had wandered over to the edge of the bluffs, and was staring up at the birds.

"Duncan?" I called. "Are you keeping a lookout?"

"Yes, Mommy," he replied, and I went back to fishing, letting my legs dangle in the cold, dark water, thinking about Andrew. I was annoyed with him for interrupting our solitude, for bringing on my nightmare, and for reminding me how much I missed adult conversation. So he'd had woman trouble. I wanted to tell him that a woman's reach never ends, that he could fly to a distant planet and her voice would echo out of the dunes, dripping sarcasm. After all, I was the woman trouble in another man's story. I'd seen that same tragic look on David's face. I used to think marriage was all about a deep understanding, in which two people became one and all secrets were known. That was a lie, and what was unknown in you began to burn after a while, like an unsolved puzzle fed to a fire.

I checked the Spam and lowered the hook in the water again. Immediately the bobber disappeared. I pulled out a catfish, bluish and more reasonably sized than the first monster I'd caught. I managed to worry the hook out of its mouth with a short stick and put the fish on a stringer I'd fashioned with some wire and the buckle from a broken belt.

"Duncan," I called. "Come see what Mommy's found."

He didn't answer.

"Duncan!"

He was at it again. He was in the business of stopping my heart. I threw my fishing rig on the bank and scrambled off the rock, and ran toward the canyon walls. "Duncan!"

"Hi, Mommy!" His voice came from high above. I stopped dead in my tracks and looked up.

"Duncan!" I screamed. He stood on a ledge fifty feet up the steep canyon wall, pointing up to a cliff swallow's nest.

"I'm almost there!" he called to me.

"Duncan, stay right there!" I ordered. "Do you hear me? Don't move!"

"What's wrong, Mommy?"

"If you move one inch, you're not ever going to come to this canyon again. Just stay there!" I had let my own son crawl up the side of a limestone cliff, and now he was in trouble. I pulled my shoes off and searched the rocks for a toehold. When I found one, I pulled myself up.

"You can do it, Mommy!" he shouted encouragingly.

"Don't move!" My hands trembled. A shrub was growing out of the wall; I tested its roots and found them strong. I pulled on the shrub with all my strength, then found another toehold and moved up another two feet. I had no idea how I was going to get my son down. I knew only that I must reach him. I closed my eyes, steadied my breathing. *I'm a negligent mother, Lord. I let my son get into this. Please help us anyway.* I kept climbing, carefully making my way up the side of the canyon, afraid to look down.

Duncan gazed at me.

"Good boy!" I shouted. "I'm coming!"

I moved my hands again, and found an indentation in a rock that I could use for a fingerhold. I set my toe in the wall and moved up, but the rock wall crumbled beneath my hand. I clawed for something to hold on to, desperately shifting the weight of my body. Then something else broke, limestone or luck, and I slid down the wall, my head hitting something hard, and the world turning black, like a catfish's eyes.

thirteen

I awoke at my own funeral, a silent, blurry, spinning affair, candlelight swirling and a choir of stalactites. I sank back under, into darkness, then rose again, glimpsing the yellow of candle flame. The pain in my head grew intense when my words formed.

"Where is he? Where is he?"

The funeral collapsed, folded in on itself, and the stalactites fell like spears, pinning me down into solid black.

fourteen

I opened my eyes. I lay on my back in the cave, on the sleeping bag. All the candles were blazing. I could look up and see the white waves on the ceiling.

"Where is he?" I asked the waves.

"You mean Duncan?"

I'd heard that voice somewhere before. I couldn't remember which world, which life. Context evaded me. A face came into my field of vision. A friendly smile, a rusty beard, and a pair of kind eyes.

"Andrew," I said.

"That's me."

"Where's my son?"

"He's right here, Martha. He's fine."

I lifted my head and looked around. Duncan sat on the side of the lake, hands crossed, looking guilty and sad.

"Oh my God. My baby. Come here, son."

Duncan knelt beside me. "I'm sorry, Mommy," he whispered. "I just wanted to see the baby birds."

I reached up to stroke his face. "Don't you know how dangerous that was? How much you scared Mommy?"

"I'm sorry."

"Okay. It's all right. Lie down next to me."

Respectful of this moment, Andrew sat cross-legged, holding a wet cloth and saying nothing. My head was throbbing, but Duncan's breath on my face drew some of the pain away. I turned toward Andrew.

"You saved us."

"No. Saving you would mean getting to you before you fell."

"Close enough."

"I heard you calling Duncan's name. I knew you were in trouble. So I started running. When I reached you, you were lying on your back, out cold."

"How did you get Duncan down?"

"Same way I used to get my cat down from the tree. I bribed him. Told him he'd get chocolate if he climbed down. Kid's got the footing of a mountain goat."

"My head is killing me."

"You might have a concussion. You should see a doctor."

"I think I do see one, over in the corner. Water is dripping off his stethoscope."

"No, really. No joking."

"How would we even get to one, out here?"

"Well, how did you get here?"

"By raft."

"You still have it?"

"I hid it in the cane. I don't even know if it would float at this point."

"We could flag down a boat."

"No. You don't understand, Andrew. I'm a fugitive. I've taken my son to a cave, and that isn't looked upon kindly in a court of law. If I'm discovered, they'll take Duncan away from me."

"I wouldn't worry about that."

"Well, I would. And I'm not going to the doctor."

"Your brain might be swelling."

"From a pea to a marble. I have room." I didn't want to talk anymore. I just wanted things to go back to the way they were a few days back, before Andrew had come into our lives. I wanted to order him out of the cave, now that I was alive and my child was safe. But my mind seemed unable to form words polite enough. He had, after all, saved us, even though one could argue that our predicament was somehow his fault, in a roundabout way, that his discovery of us soured our luck. I didn't tell him to go. Instead I closed my eyes and rested, my head falling over until it touched Duncan's. The candlelight was warm. The aching in my head beat down to the pulse of a baby cliff swallow, rapid and faint, and I slept.

It must have been the fear of wasted candlelight that awakened me. My head still hurt, but my vision was clear. I gently released Duncan, who was fast asleep, and crawled around the cave, snuffing out candles and enjoying the tiny scent each smoking wick released. I left the candles around the lake burning, and also around Andrew; he slept in the lotus position next to a rock, his head tilted to the right. His skin was shining, and candlelight had found a hole in his shirt and lit up the circle of skin.

His head came up from one shoulder and slumped down toward the other. He crossed his arms in his sleep, stretched a leg out. And what of Andrew's own history? Something must have driven him here. What if he had his own bad dreams, and it turned out that nightmares were shared in this cave, like oxygen and music? I didn't want his nightmares. I'd journeyed a thousand miles and broken every law to lose my own.

But I couldn't make him go. I needed him. And yes, maybe he'd made me need him, in the same way that knives and cotton came into primitive tribes and demanded to be needed, but here he was, and I had almost killed my son today, out of nothing but rank negligence. I realized, with a deep ache, that even in the desert, events were unpredictable. Duncan and I could live forever out here without another mishap; or tomorrow something terrible could happen suddenly, out of the blue. Andrew, a man who possibly brought the need for a savior as well as the saving itself, could help me watch over my son. That was the gift he could bring, in return for his cost.

Andrew opened his eyes. "How do you feel?" he asked quietly, in deference to my sleeping son, or my aching head.

"My head still hurts. But less."

"Good." He rubbed his beard.

"You told me yesterday that you would leave. But you didn't."

"You needed me. You were over your head out here."

"All mothers are over their heads. The trick is pretending we're not." I looked down at Duncan, who was still sound asleep. Giving his mother both a heart attack and a possible concussion must have tired him out. "I wish you hadn't come here, Andrew."

"Do you want me to leave?"

"Would you really leave?"

"Yes."

I noticed his knapsack, set on a shelf of rock as though it belonged there. "No, you wouldn't leave. You've already bullied your way into our lives and invited all those random events. You'll hang around the area, unseen, until the next time we fall off a cliff or a buzzard carries off my son or a grizzly bear comes down from Alaska and starts to eat us. Then you'll save us from something that would have just been the time of day if you'd never been here at all."

"You sound like you think I've ruined everything. And that's the last thing I ever wanted to do."

"I'm being ungrateful. You saved me today. You saved my boy. You hear those stories about women losing their children and somehow carrying on with life? That's their choice, not mine. I refuse to live without my son. If he died today, I'd die too."

"You must love him very much."

"I love him too much. And I make no apologies."

He looked around. "You've blown out some of the candles."

"You were splurging on light."

His gaze rested on the lake, whose surface still shone. "You left the lake lit."

"It looked so pretty, I thought you might like waking up and seeing it."

"You're right about that." He rose, then vanished briefly into darkness before reemerging at the side of the lake. "Is the water cold?" he asked from across the chamber.

"Not if you pretend it isn't. Duncan and I go in there all the time."

"What's it like?"

"Like swimming in a fairy tale. Go ahead. Climb in."

He hesitated, then unbuttoned his shirt and slid it off. His torso was rangy, his muscles lean and tight. What if Duncan had fallen from that bluff? Would Andrew have had the strength to catch him? I watched as he removed his pants. The shedding of his clothes seemed to radiate his scent. He did a half-turn and pulled off his shorts, exposing the side of his pale flank. I caught my breath, surprised. Had Miss Manners burrowed into a cave, she would have called this nudity inappropriate. But she was far away, back in a land full of rules and violence.

Andrew slid into the lake, and I rose and walked through the shadows to sit in the candlelight and watch him swim. The blind fish darted away from him, the muscles tensed in his back, his bare feet kicked. He came to the surface and let his breath out, shaking his head so that drops of cool water hit my arms and face.

"It's pretty damn cold. But it's serene." He sank back down in the water until it came to his chin. "I can see how you didn't want anyone to find you here."

I said nothing.

"Is there someone in particular who wants to find you?"

"Like who?"

"Like a husband?"

"Your nudity is fine. Your nosiness is rude."

"I'm sorry." He went back under the water by way of apology, then resurfaced.

"I'll answer you, Andrew," I said. "I guess it doesn't matter.

I have a husband. His name is David and he lives in Ohio. We separated over issues of belief."

"You mean, which church to attend?"

"If it were only that simple."

"You think he's looking for you?"

"I know it. And it makes me nervous, because once he sets his mind to something, there's no stopping him."

"Do you still love him?"

"Yes, I do. The love has done nicely out here. It's become quite bearable, actually. Of course, I don't feel very good about keeping Duncan away from his father."

He nodded. "A boy needs his daddy, that's for sure."

"My husband thinks I'm crazy. That's hard to live with. Imagine the person you love, thinking that about you."

He put his hands flat on the water and swept them in a slow arc. "You're not crazy."

"How do you know?"

"You just don't sound like crazy women are supposed to sound."

"And how do they sound?"

"Like my ex-wife. How's your head?"

"Better."

"You don't feel sick?"

"No. Every now and again the candlelight moves funny, and the cave does a little turn, like a merry-go-round. But my mind is clear. Unless you're really not naked. Then I'm in trouble."

"Maybe you're okay. I don't know. I'm not a doctor."

"What are you?"

"Nothing, really. And I don't want to be anything. At least, not for a while."

The inside of my arm felt tight. Looking down, I saw a bruise growing, the pink fringes of it climbing the knobby part of my wrist. "Let's get back to the issue of your staying or not staying, shall we?"

"All right."

"Do you have nightmares?"

"Sometimes."

"That's rule one. No nightmares in here. They disturb the bats."

"All right. No nightmares."

"And you must help me protect my son from any danger, any harm. This is how you will earn your keep."

"I will help you protect your son."

"And third, you have to help us hide from my husband."

He looked at me solemnly, raised one wet hand.

fifteen

I awakened to find the pebbles of our calendar had been taken from their little pile and had begun to form a circle around our sleeping bags. Andrew was already up. His back to me, he was busy at the Coleman stove; we were starting to run out of propane. My head still hurt from the fall, and I blinked rapidly a few times to see if Andrew would disappear. But he remained in place, shirtless, busy, the candlelight revealing a group of moles in the middle of his back.

"Andrew?"

He turned his head. "Ah. You're awake. I was afraid you'd succumbed to your head injury during the night, and then, well, we'd have to bury you."

"That's very sweet."

Duncan stirred, turned over on his stomach, and went back to sleep.

"Why did you rearrange our calendar around our sleeping bags?" I asked Andrew.

He didn't answer right away. He was pouring hot water from a tin pot into two mugs. "Protection," he said, and reached for the jar of instant coffee and unscrewed the lid.

"A bunch of rocks are going to protect us?"

"Have a little faith. They're magic rocks. Of course, they'll achieve their full power when the circle is complete."

I looked over at his sleeping bag by the lake.

"What's going to protect you?"

"My natural charm."

"Oh. So you'll die terribly."

He stirred the powdered coffee into the mugs and handed one to me.

"It's so strange," I told him. "Waking up to find you here. And you've already figured out where the coffee is, you've already taken over the counting of days. This isn't how I imagined it all turning out."

"How did you imagine it?"

I shrugged. "Rocks. Water. Peace."

"You've still got that," he said, but I wasn't sure. He set down his mug and crossed the chamber to the lake, where he knelt and washed his face. Duncan sat up and rubbed his eyes, and gazed at Andrew.

"He's still here?" Duncan asked.

"Yes, baby."

Duncan threw his arms around me and held me tight. "Thank you, Mommy," he whispered. "Thank you."

. . .

Andrew and I faced upriver, the morning light soft and the rock still cool against our bare legs, as Duncan moved in and out among the boulders, chasing a brown lizard.

"He hasn't caught one yet, poor boy," I said. "They're too fast for him."

"What are?" Andrew asked.

"The lizards."

"I'll catch one."

"No, it's a challenge for him. We didn't have those kinds of lizards back in Ohio. Plenty of squirrels, though."

Andrew gazed up the river. "So this is the lookout rock, huh?"

"It works pretty well. You don't find many people traveling this far on foot. A man came by on a horse, once. Every day I look up that river, and I wonder, is this going to be the day that I see my husband come floating by on a raft? Part of me thinks there's no way he'd ever find us. But he's a determined man, and very smart."

Andrew drew his knees up to his chest. "He's not so smart, if he let you get away."

A lizard appeared on top of a nearby boulder, and Duncan's head came into view and his predatory eyes narrowed. I saw his hand come up steadily, quietly. The lizard made a sudden leap onto a stalk of lechuguilla, and Duncan's hand came down on the rock too late.

"Ahh!" he shouted, and I laughed.

"What are you laughing at?" Andrew asked, turning to me.

"Duncan. He's got his father's stalking genes."

"Let me ask you something. You yourself admit that you love

your husband. What would be so terrible, if he did find you and Duncan?"

"First of all, something's happened to him. He's not in his right mind, and Duncan can't be around that. Secondly, he'd take us back to Ohio, and it's not safe."

"Ohio's not safe?"

"You don't know, do you? I guess you were already out here when it happened."

"When what happened?"

Just then Duncan ran up to me, blond hair flying in all directions. "Did you see, Mommy?" he asked, huffing and puffing. "I almost caught him!"

"You were very close, honey," I said, but Duncan was already back to the hunt, stalking creatures that were used to spending the late mornings drowsing on the rocks but now were fugitives, darting for their lives.

I knew Andrew was waiting for me to continue the story, but I said nothing.

"You know what's funny?" he said at last. "You ran away from your husband, and my wife ran away from me. I wonder if your husband was as surprised as I was, the morning I woke up and found the house empty."

"You didn't see it coming?"

"Hell, no. I really thought she was happy. I mean, we had our ups and downs, like any other couple. I'd had a change in jobs, but I thought she'd like it that I was around the house a little more. She never complained. Never sat me down and said, 'Listen, this is going to have to change, or I'm out of here.' Believe me, I would have listened if she had. Instead she pretended that everything was fine, and meanwhile she was setting up her new life."

"Was there someone else?"

"Not then, I don't think. I've got to tell you, this is how much of an idiot I was. I was proud of the husband I was to her. It was really the only thing I thought I'd done right in my life. And one morning she's gone and there's a note basically saying that I'd done nothing right. Everything was wrong. Even my love for her was wrong. And what does a man do then, if his love is all wrong? How does he fix that? And tell me, what use is a man who can't seem to get this basic principle right? That's like a man who can't drink water." His voice had grown tight. He lowered his eyes.

"How long has it been?"

"Five years."

"You're divorced now?"

"Yes. Next time I saw her, we were in court. She ended up marrying someone else and having a couple of kids. I always wanted kids. I would have given anything to have a little boy, just like yours."

"I'm sorry. I can see how you'd want to get away from her memory."

Andrew leaned back on his elbows and looked up at the sky. "I don't know how possible it is to truly forget anything."

"Well, someone once told me that out here, anything is possible. Just like your friend told you."

He glanced over at me. "You think you can forget about this husband of yours?"

"I don't know. I love him more than anyone in the world. Except Duncan, of course. I feel that he left me no choice."

"But did you really try to talk to him?" Andrew asked earnestly. "Did you really try to work it out?"

"Listen, our stories are totally different. Trust me."

He shook his head. "You're an interesting person, Martha. Not bad-looking either."

"Hey." I held up my ring so that it glinted in the light. "Don't get any ideas. I'm a married woman."

"Don't worry. I'm not interested in you."

"You're not? Why not?"

"You're crazy."

"Last night you said I wasn't crazy!"

"I needed a place to sleep. But you, woman, are as crazy as a loon." He got up and flapped his arms, danced around. "Aaa-hooo!" he called. "Aaahoooooo!"

Duncan was winding up for another pounce at a lizard, but at the sound of Andrew's voice he froze, intrigued.

"Look, Duncan," I called, pointing at Andrew. "It's a bird."

By midafternoon the sun was broiling in the sky, and we were forced to take refuge in the shade of the salt cedar trees, where we lounged together, bored.

"That's the hardest thing about this place," I said, rubbing two sticks together idly. "Finding ways to entertain Duncan. That's why we risk going down to the river every day. Duncan loves it so much."

Andrew looked at my sticks. "I know a trick Duncan might like."

"Show me the trick!" cried Duncan. "Show me! Show me!"

"Now you've done it," I said. "He was almost asleep ten seconds ago."

"He'll like this," Andrew said, rising to his feet. He found a slender branch and bent it into the shape of a bow, then tied it into position with a lace from his hiking boot. He scavenged pieces of wood in varying shapes, and with his pocketknife carved a depression into a flat piece of mesquite. Duncan and I watched as he whittled another piece of wood down to what looked like a drill, and cut a notch in the side of the mesquite. He whistled a bit as he worked, something I recognized as a John Denver tune. Duncan began to whistle too, imitating him.

When Andrew had finished whittling, he threaded the bow onto the homemade drill, put his foot on the board, and rapidly moved the bow back and forth, spinning the drill around until a thread of smoke rose from the side notch. I saw the flare of a single red ember.

Duncan gasped and I felt a little jealous. This was the kind of miracle a mother couldn't perform. Ours were softer: knitted sweaters and risen bread and headache remedies.

"Want to see a cross-stitch, Duncan?" I asked.

He ignored me.

Andrew blew on the ember, adding a small amount of dried cottonwood fibers. Duncan leaned in close, helping him blow.

"Not too hard, Duncan," I warned.

The tinder burst into flame, and Duncan gave out a short, worshipful yelp.

"Andrew," I said, "I had matches."

"You are such a woman." He sprinkled some twigs on the new fire. "There you go."

"How did you learn to do that?"

"That's the only thing I did right in Eagle Scouts—I got a badge for it. I was the fire-maker. It was a big hit with the Girl Scouts in the next camp. The secret is the blowing. You must seduce the ember. Make it feel like becoming a flame is its own idea rather than yours."

"So you are a master at seduction?" I teased.

"Oh, yes."

"I can tell," I said, "given your luck with women."

He looked at me quickly, and I saw the hurt in his eyes. "I'm sorry, Andrew. I was kidding." I gathered a handful of twigs and offered them in a gesture of atonement.

Andrew kept the fire going the rest of the afternoon, and that night he transferred it to the cave.

"Be careful," I told him. "This cave has good ventilation. But you've got to watch the smoke." Andrew, though, turned out to be a master of cave fire. He fed it until our side of the chamber was so bright we didn't even need candles.

"I'm an Indian!" Duncan announced, breaking into a war whoop and dancing around the fire.

After Duncan had exhausted himself with his Indian dance and flopped onto the floor, Andrew took a bottle from his knapsack and poured something into a cup. He offered it to me. "Want some?"

"What is it?"

"Whiskey."

"No, thanks. I don't really drink. Every once in a while I'll have a strawberry daiquiri, but that's it."

"Can't help you there," he said, and came to sit down next to me.

"This is the best night ever," Duncan said, holding his hands out to the fire. "Let's play Flashlight Stories!"

"All right," I said agreeably. I found the flashlight and shined the beam away from the fire, at a formation in a far corner. "Look, it's a jackrabbit, and he's very lonely. The other jack-rabbits don't like him because he only has one ear. . . ." The flashlight moved in tiny increments as I described the jackrabbit's life and how it all turned around when he met the one-legged weasel who lived on the other side of the meadow, a weasel who understood all too well the pain involved in being beautiful only on the inside. Too late, I realized my mistake. The love story was boring my son.

"I want Andrew to tell me a story!" Duncan cried.

I handed the flashlight to Andrew. "It's your turn. I think I lost him when the jackrabbit kissed the one-legged weasel, which I modeled after a scene from *Casablanca.*"

Andrew looked doubtful. "I don't know much about telling stories," he said, but he took the flashlight and moved it around the cave until it stopped to illuminate a nest of calcite. "Once there was a prince who was turned into a frog . . ." The beam moved. ". . . by an evil witch. The problem was, the prince had this beautiful stallion that was so grief-stricken by the loss of his prince that he decided to run away. So the stallion ran into the enchanted forest—"

The beam darted suddenly into the thicket of stalagmites. Duncan clapped.

"—and so the frog took off in hot pursuit. . . . Wait a minute. What's that?" The beam had found one of Duncan's army men. Andrew crawled toward the forest, guided by the flashlight. He reached in and took the army man out, inspecting it under the light, the beam so close I expected the little green man to melt. "Oh my gosh!" Andrew exclaimed. "The army man just decided to join the navy! Man overboard! Man overboard!" He ran to the edge of the lake and I heard a tiny splash.

"We must save him, Duncan!" Andrew shouted. "We must save him from the gigantic blind soldier-eating fish!" He slid into the lake fully clothed, and disappeared.

"The fish are coming! The fish are coming!" Duncan howled, rushing across the room and throwing himself in the lake after Andrew.

"You two have violated every rule of Flashlight Stories," I scolded, but I went to the water's edge to see them swimming together, as the blind fish scattered, terrified by the introduction of horseplay. I hadn't seen my son so happy in weeks. Andrew came to the surface to take a breath and caught me looking at him.

"Flashlight Stories prohibits the use of props," I said. "You cheated your way past my one-legged weasel and I hate you."

He held out his arms. "Water's freezing. Come on in."

sixteen

I stood under the tree, craning my neck, bracing myself to catch my son.

"Don't," he said from his perch on the cottonwood branch. "I don't need you to catch me."

The new day was coming. Pink light eased over the mountain range. Apparently Andrew's spirited flashlight tale had set off Duncan's latest dream of flight: I had caught him sneaking out of the cave before dawn to try out his new wings without me.

"I wish we had a camera," Duncan said. "You could take a picture of me flying."

"Come on, honey. Just jump. My arms are hurting."

He took his position, his bare toes gripping the branch. He looked up at the pink sky, narrowed his eyes, and jumped. His eyes went wide, and we fell to the ground in a heap.

"Ohhh," Duncan sighed, his chest contracting in my arms as his breath escaped. He pulled himself from my grasp, went over to the tree and kicked it. "Stupid tree!"

"What do you think you're doing?" I heard Andrew ask.

I looked up and saw him coming toward us.

"Duncan had his flying dream again," I explained, and pointed to the branch. "That's his liftoff pad. He jumps and I catch him."

"Ah, Duncan," said Andrew. "I was watching. Your technique is all wrong. Let me try it."

I got to my feet and brushed myself off. "I'm not catching you."

"Why would you need to catch me, if I'm going to fly? Move back, woman, and let me show Duncan how it's done."

"You'll break your neck."

"You of little faith." He hoisted himself up on a tree limb and grabbed the one over his head, pulling himself up. It bent under him.

"I don't think that can support your weight," I said.

"In Boy Scouts, they used to call me Tarzan," Andrew said. "I was a champion tree-climber." He moved his feet apart, getting his balance, then let go of the limb above him. "All it takes—"

I heard a giant crack, and the limb broke under him, sending him sprawling onto the ground.

"Andrew!" I shrieked. Duncan and I ran over and knelt beside him. "Are you all right?" I asked.

Andrew opened his eyes and stared up at the sky. "That was

the most beautiful flight," he said. "The birds were so nice to me. And the clouds were so fluffy."

Duncan fell on the ground and rolled back and forth, howling with laughter. I hadn't heard my son laugh like that since before Linda died.

The other advantages of having Andrew around soon made themselves known. We had fresh fish every night. We had a towel rack, made out of cane, and shoes woven from palmetto. We had a stove made of stone. And Duncan had a friend on his lookout rock; together the two of them stared up the river, alert for intruders, Duncan now aware that this role was a brave one and that he had never quite appreciated it before. As they watched in silence, Duncan copied Andrew's posture. I could see my son gaining confidence day by day. He walked with a little swagger. He was no longer a boy who cried for his father; he was the prince of lost places, captain of the river, master of the cave. And even the memory of a bossy little girl was letting him go, her attributes scattering among the offerings of the desert: beautiful birds, elusive lizards, argumentative squirrels. A river that could never be tamed.

Duncan started attending classes every afternoon near a cluster of lechuguilla, on a patch of cleared earth. I taught him spelling, carving each letter into the hard ground with the sharp end of a stick, and the ground was soon covered with words. Rabbit. Boy. Girl. Duck. Red. Fish. Jump. Egg. Glass. Sad. Duncan learned so many words that within a week we started running out of earth. Whole sentences would mean we had to conquer new lands, displace ancient peoples.

Flashlight Stories at night served as a reward for good spelling in the afternoon. As Duncan sat still, enthralled, Andrew sipped at his tin cup and slowly undid my ordinary tales. What had once been a hawk swooping down on a man eating pretzels became a pirate turning good and claiming a kingdom. Monsters interrupted chess games to do battle, and be defeated by a tribe of fairies enslaved for centuries by the dark god of a bell-shaped planet. And a wolf story couldn't stay the same; Andrew changed it before the water did, drips of calcite speeding up a million centuries until the wolf battled enemies the cave hadn't grown yet.

Even John Denver was coming back to life, which seemed impossible, as the batteries in the CD player had been dead for days. But his voice filled the cave; and maybe John Denver was dead only in my memory. Remove that memory and throw it in the lake; let it sink to the bottom and suddenly his plane gains altitude. His engine lives.

I worried about how much Andrew drank from his cup, and I wondered if his knapsack held only bottles of liquor, an endless and magical supply that would keep his eyes red forever. But I said nothing. He had brought my boy back to life, and I was grateful for that. And having him in the cave made it easier for me not to think about David, although images of him did intrude, and I wondered if our trail had gone cold for him, if he'd given up. But of course I knew he hadn't; it wasn't David's way. And even if I was to know, truly, that he'd moved on without us, it would devastate me. Deep down, I still held out hope that someday he would come to his senses.

Every now and then I caught Andrew looking at me, the expression on his face unmistakable. It seemed only natural that a cave could corral a man and a woman and keep them in the dark until they fell in love. But I fought against it. I was still a married woman, and I still loved David, although I felt myself blushing one night when Andrew suddenly told a flashlight story about the fervent love between a golden mermaid and a magic frog, a story so romantic that Duncan fell asleep.

seventeen

All I wanted was a decent pair of scissors and a mirror. Instead I sat on a rock and cut my hair with the miniature scissors of a Swiss Army knife. A dry wind caught the pieces of hair and flung them in the direction of the river. My hands shook a little as I worked.

"Good morning," said Andrew, approaching me. "Beauty makeover?" he asked.

"I'm sick of my hair," I answered. "It's too long to wear in the desert. Drives me crazy in the heat of the afternoon."

"Well, you're making a real mess of it."

"Who asked you?"

He smiled tolerantly. "You know, I think I know you well

enough to notice that when you're upset about something, you throw yourself into a project."

"Why would I be upset?"

"You violated a sacred rule last night."

"What rule?"

"No nightmares."

I sighed. So he had heard me. I put the knife down in my lap and let my breath out.

"Let me help you." He took the knife from me and went to work himself. "See?" he said. "You've got to do just a few strands at a time, with this stupid little pair of scissors. How much do you want off?"

"Four inches."

"That much?" I didn't answer him; I just sat there trying to wish the memory of my nightmare away as his fingers moved gently through my hair and the sun rose in the sky. He hummed as he worked, his song soothing me. I couldn't quite place it—a lullaby, or something from *The Wizard of Oz.* Blond tendrils fell to the ground and crawled down the bluff like wispy creatures too frail to face the rising sun. Finally Andrew stopped combing and snipping.

"I think it looks pretty good," he said.

I ran my fingers through my hair. "The ends feel even. You're a great hairstylist."

"I'm gay."

"When's the last time you cut your own hair? It's looking kind of shaggy."

"I don't know. It's been a while. I used to wear it short, above my ears, but I'm getting used to it this way. Maybe I'll let it grow down to my waist and turn hippie."

"Why don't you let me cut it?"

He hesitated.

"All right. If it would make you feel better."

We changed places and I set to work, snipping his rust-colored curls as he closed his eyes. It felt good to touch his hair. I moved around him in circles, pressing in close to him. Once he rested his hand on the back of my calf, and removed it only when I stopped cutting. In twenty-five minutes, he was a man with a short, uneven cut. I stood back, looking at my handiwork.

"Well?" he said.

"It looks good."

"Really?"

"You can ask Duncan when he comes out, but let me talk to him first." I studied him some more. "Do you have a razor?"

"Yes, but—"

"Get it. Let me shave you. Your beard looks funny, now that your hair is so short."

He gave me a look I didn't quite understand. "I don't know about that," he said. "I've tried to shave it off before, and it doesn't really look right."

"It would look right to me."

He put his hand protectively against his right cheek. "It's a bigger deal than you think. But I'll make you a deal. I'll let you shave me if you tell me about your nightmare."

I hesitated, but I knew the time had come to tell him the whole story. "Deal," I said finally.

Andrew disappeared inside the cave, then returned with a straight razor and a pan of water from the lake.

I took the razor from him. "Do you have any shaving cream?"

"No." He brandished a tube of aloe vera lotion. "We'll have to use this." He sat down and I started trimming his beard with the scissors.

"What did I say last night?" I asked.

"Not much. You were moaning in your sleep. I almost woke you up."

Whiskers gathered on his jeans as I worked. "There was a little girl who used to live next door to us. Duncan loved her. Her name was Linda." I paused, waiting for the pain, but felt only the sun warming my back. "She and Duncan went to school together. I put them on the bus every day. There was a janitor at the school, no one you'd ever pay attention to." I dipped my hands into the pan and spread the cool water on the stubble of Andrew's cheeks, dabbed on the lotion, and began to shave him, starting at his left ear and moving the razor cautiously down toward his chin. "And this janitor had a perfect attendance record and treated his old mother very well. But he had a grudge against something or someone, or maybe everyone. One day he went to school like any other day, he washed down the halls like he did every day, only on this day . . ." I took the razor away from Andrew's face, afraid that my next words would cause him to jerk and make me cut him.

"On this day he had a bomb in his mop bucket."

Andrew looked into my eyes, a wide patch of new pale skin showing where the razor had scraped. "My God," he said.

I paused to wash the razor in the water, then knelt to scrape his chin before I continued the story. "And Linda was killed, right in front of Duncan's eyes."

"I didn't know," he said. "I must have been out here."

"How lucky to stay clean like that when the rest of the nation was getting dirty."

I wet the other side of his face, softened his beard with the lotion, and started shaving again.

"How many kids died?"

"Just Linda. Nine others were injured."

"Did they catch the janitor?"

"He blew up too."

"But why did he do it? There must have been a reason."

"He left a letter. Said something about how he would have taken every child in the world with him, if he could have. And that he had no regrets. Died with a smile on his face, I'm sure."

A bit of beard remained along the side of Andrew's face. He clasped my wrist for a moment, stopping me. Before I could speak he let the wrist go, and I finished the last part, a scar taking shape under the razor. I wet my fingers and cleaned the lotion away. The scar emerged whole, shaped like a leaf and slightly purple in the light. I stroked it with my fingertips.

"This is what you didn't want me to see?"

"It's ugly."

"I don't think so. I don't think so at all. A healed wound is beautiful, if you ask me." I leaned in close and kissed the scar, felt its rough texture under my lips, and then I was looking into Andrew's eyes. He put his hands on the sides of my face.

"I'm so sorry, Martha." Tears were forming in his eyes, surprising me. "I'm sorry. I'm sorry."

I touched his scar again. "Don't you see why I had to bring Duncan out here? How could he live in that world? Forty million mothers would have followed me out here, if they had known this place existed."

eighteen

The desert was playing tricks on him again. Just that morning he had counted the pebbles around the sleeping bags and found, to his amazement, that seventeen days had passed since he had first come to the cave. Astonished, he made another count, then another. He would have guessed ten days, at most. Now he sat with his head against the trunk of a salt cedar tree and sipped from his tin cup. Salt cedars were the pests of the desert, robbing the water table of a hundred gallons a day. He knew something about unquenchable thirst.

His last bottle was half empty; his hands trembled at the thought of running out. He had to get back to town, stock up on a new supply, call the distraught husband in Ohio and tell him what he'd found. Each night he planned to take the trip in the morning. And then the next day would pass, disorienting him. Suddenly night would fall, and he would be back in the cave, shining a flashlight on fantastic stories. And lately, after all the lights were off, save one burning candle, he would see things. Flashes of a figure in a corner of the chamber, increasingly real. But it couldn't be.

He shook his head and took a sip of nothing but dry desert air. The cup was empty and had been, perhaps, for some time. Surely he couldn't be drinking enough to see what he saw. And deep down, he knew that the desert was just sand and shadows and hot pulp buried under the endless thorns, and even when mixed with whiskey could not account for his confusion. It was the woman's spell. A woman who grew more beautiful every day, and more sane as his own sanity declined. He had found a tuft of her hair caught in a blooming bush and had saved it, kept it under a corner of his sleeping bag, and sometimes he woke up with it inside his clenched fist.

He had come to her a liar, a man hired for the job of deceit. Pretend to be a different man, in the desert to escape a bad marriage, rather than do the job of a hunter. Pretend to love John Denver when he was a Tom Waits man. Take the name of her beloved father and earn her trust. But he found himself telling her the truth in unexpected places. He had meant to use the tale of his ex-wife to make her feel guilty about leaving her own husband, yet the story unraveled from its fixed purpose and suddenly he was telling her the truth as he knew it. The fierce pain and haunting sense of failure. And the fact that love had proven to be a useless tool; a lighter drained of fluid, or a knife that loses its point in the soft flesh of a cactus. Even his new name, Andrew, seemed to fit him better than the old one. Sometimes he forgot what the old name was.

Of course he'd known about the janitor and the bomb and the dead child. But to hear the story through a mother's point of view horrified him, as if he had stumbled on it for the first time, and he wanted to throw his arms around her and protect her from the story, bury it forever with a thousand stories about pirates and magic cats.

"Andrew," he said out loud, testing the name. He rested the empty cup against his knee and watched the sky turn colors, orange and pink and yellow. Soon the chill of evening would come, pushing its darker themes of violet and red.

"There you are." He looked up. She was standing over him, wearing a pair of light blue shorts. "I've been looking all over for you. What are you doing?"

"Thinking," he said. "What are you doing?"

She reached down, brushed the dirt from her knees. "Teaching Duncan the word 'boat.'"

"How about 'existentialism'?"

"You're thinking of the advanced class, one cactus over." She sat down next to him, and he thought he caught a hint of an aroma that reminded him of violets.

"Are you wearing cologne?"

She laughed. "Are you crazy? Why would I be wearing cologne out here?"

She turned around so that they faced each other, their knees touching, and he felt a pang of guilt, sitting here betraying two people: the man who'd hired him and the woman who trusted him. He had to choose one soon, not just a side but a perspective. A way of thinking. A belief.

"I want to tell you something, Martha."

She looked at him calmly, and he almost told her everything. The whole truth. But what if this truth caused him to lose her?

He wasn't so good at predicting what would make a woman leave.

"I want you to know," he said, "that if I could have taken that bomb out to a field and held it in my arms until it went off, if I could have spared those children, I would have done that in a second." He felt his eyes go wet again. He picked up his tin cup and found a gulp of whiskey that had somehow been hiding from him.

"You know what I think about sometimes, Andrew? That old woman, the janitor's mother. She was asleep when he did it. I imagine her lying on a daybed, a shawl over her legs, the sunlight coming through the window. She must have looked so peaceful."

She leaned in to him and put her head on his shoulder, and he held her like that, watching the colors of the sky, picturing her arranging flowers in a vase in her shop, as the bomb went off on the other side of town.

nineteen

Duncan stared at the word "knife" and shook his head.

"Come on," I urged. "Sound it out."

He looked at the ground doubtfully. "Kife."

"No, Duncan. You see, letters sometimes change when you put them together. *K* and *n* sound like *n.* See?" I found a flat rock and smoothed out all the other words, leaving a blank slate on which to put the exceptions of the world, the oddities. Knob. Know. Knuckle. Knee. I was just about to prepare my son for the act of God that is the *ph* sound, when Andrew appeared, breathless before us, his bare feet ruining the lesson. We looked up at him in surprise.

He grabbed my hand. "Come with me. You won't believe this."

twenty

Comanche Indians used to roam these canyons, using cinnabar for war paint. Gazing down the bluff at the tents by the river, we were those Indians; we had that same outraged sense of violation. I had left Duncan sitting in his stone classroom with orders not to move from his spelling lesson while Andrew and I climbed down for a closer look, careful to remain unseen. We ducked behind a rock formation and peered out cautiously. A raucous group, several men and just as many women, drank beer and played loud music. Two giant rafts had been pulled to the bank. A big red dog wandered around lawn chairs set up in a circle, the bell on its collar tinkling. The men looked to be in their early twenties, and wore brightly colored shorts, and thongs on their feet. Their stomachs shone white in the sun as they applied sunscreen. There was something outrageous about their manner, something sloppy and unappreciative. An inclination to litter, or make camp on young ferns.

"I want them to leave, Andrew," I whispered.

But they stayed, on to the next day, and the next. We could no longer swim in our favorite place in the river, or walk down the banks. We were afraid, even, to wander very far from the cave.

"We're prisoners," I said.

"They'll leave on their own, sooner or later," Andrew replied.

"They scare me, Andrew. What if that stupid dog finds us? And of course, Duncan's so curious I'm afraid he'll slip out of the cave one night and go investigate."

Indeed, Duncan spent his waking moments crouched behind bushes or hidden behind rocks, watching them. The dog especially fascinated him. "I want a dog. A big red one, like him."

On the third night I grew frantic. "What are we going to do?" I demanded.

"We can move to another cave," said Andrew. His whiskey had run out earlier that day, and a certain tension filled his voice.

"Another cave?" Duncan asked, delighted. "There are other caves? Why didn't you tell me before?"

"We aren't moving," I said firmly. "This is the old man's cave, and we're staying. We're just going to have to think of a way to get those people out of here."

"There is one way," Andrew said.

"What?"

"They've got a big cooler full of food. We steal the food, they have to leave."

After Duncan fell asleep, Andrew and I crept down to the camp, and I waited for him in a patch of carrizo cane by the river, careful not to step in ants again. The campers had finished their drinking and card-playing. Their tents were quiet. The air was cool, and the cane made a rushing sound that frightened me in these circumstances. I crouched and hugged my knees, wishing I hadn't insisted on coming. I had thought I could help. Now I realized that my presence here was only a liability, something Andrew had to worry about when his mind should have been wholly on theft.

I heard his footsteps and started to rise out of the cane to greet him. But then I heard something else that made me duck down.

The tinkling of a bell.

I tried not to move, but my legs trembled. The footsteps came closer and faltered, and I heard a low, drunken curse, a zipper being undone, and the sound of someone peeing at the edge of the cane. I held my breath until the peeing stopped.

"Binky," said a man's voice, and the dog's head appeared in the cane right in front of my face. I gasped. The dog growled, baring its teeth at me.

"Binky?" Now the man himself crashed into the cane with us, his eyes flying open in surprise when he saw me.

I jumped to my feet, but the man seized my arm. "Wait!" he said. "Who are you?"

I forgot myself. "Andrew! Andrew!"

The man's grip tightened and he pulled me toward him, his grasp strong despite his drunken condition. The dog began barking loudly.

"Don't!" I said, and then another person entered the cane and leapt on the drunk man.

"Andrew!" I gasped.

They struggled wildly in the cane, the dog howling now, and voices coming from the camp.

Andrew punched the man, and he groaned. He hit him again, and when the man fell, Andrew leapt on him, hitting him over and over.

I grabbed Andrew's shoulder. "Stop it! That's enough!" I pulled him off the man, and we ran out of the cane and down the side of the riverbank, the drunk man suddenly screaming in unearthly howls.

Flashlights behind us. A stitch in my side. Andrew pulled me into the river, and the water splashed up to my knees. We waded to a boulder and sank down, chest-deep in the water. We could see flashlights along the bank.

"Don't move," Andrew whispered in my ear, his arms around me. "Just stay quiet."

"What's the matter with you?"

"I said be quiet."

"You hurt that man!"

"Shut up!"

"They went that way!" the drunk man shouted.

"Who were they?" someone demanded.

"Shit. I don't know. There were two of 'em."

"Get 'em, Binky!"

Binky the Big Red Dog paused to sniff at our footprints on the bank and then rushed past our boulder and on down the river. The voices continued for an hour as we waited silently in the water. Finally we heard someone say, "Hell, I'm going to bed." In a few minutes, all was quiet.

"I think they went to bed," Andrew whispered.

My heart was still beating fast. "I can't take this. This can't happen out here."

"It's okay. You're safe. Did that guy hurt you?"

"Just my arm, where he grabbed it." I showed him my arm and he tried to inspect it under moonlight.

"I'm sorry," he said at last. "I'm so sorry."

He kissed my wrist and pulled me to my feet, and we made our way back to the cave, dripping water on the cool stones.

The next morning the campers had disappeared, having left everything they didn't want. Styrofoam cups, empty beer cans, empty bags of chips, sandwich wrappers. The three of us walked through their camp, kicking at the litter. I wanted to ask Andrew why he'd been so crazy last night, but I didn't dare.

"Those people are litterbugs," Duncan said, reaching for a paper bag.

"Don't touch that!" I warned him. "Don't touch anything!" I looked at Andrew. "I guess you scared them off."

"I bet you anything the men wanted to stay," Andrew said. "But I probably scared the women."

"What do we do now? Do you think they'll call the Rangers?"

He shrugged. "I'm telling you, I think we should make a move."

He said it again back in the cave, as he poured whiskey from a half-empty bottle that looked different from the others I'd seen.

"Where did you get that?" I asked.

"Found it at their camp."

"Well, I guess something good came of this."

He caught my tone and drank deeply. In a few minutes I saw the old Andrew return, gentle and sweet. "Don't worry about it, Martha." He tapped his fingers on the side of his tin cup. "I'll make this last." But he didn't. It was gone by nightfall, and the next day when I awoke he had already strapped on his knapsack.

"Are we moving?" Duncan said eagerly.

"Where are you going?" I asked Andrew.

He chose to answer my question rather than Duncan's. "Just back into town. I'll be right back."

"Right back? It'll take you a couple of days, at least."

"I need to get some supplies."

"What kind of supplies, Andrew?"

He didn't answer me, so I picked up a bottle. "These supplies?"

"None of your business," he said, and his voice wasn't so friendly anymore.

"I want to go to town!" Duncan shouted, jumping up and down. "I want candy and I want chocolate and I want—"

"So let me get this straight," I said to Andrew, in a tone that made Duncan stand still. "You would leave my son and me here alone, after I was attacked, to go get whiskey."

"You don't understand. You don't understand anything!"

I gathered up his four empty bottles and dropped them in the lake. "If you leave, then don't come back."

"Martha . . ."

I folded my arms. "I mean it. Don't come back."

He moved to a place where he was too tall for the candlelight to reach, and his footsteps faded away.

Duncan started after him, but I took his arm. "Don't you dare."

We were alone again, the pebbles stretching half a circle around our sleeping bags. "He'll be back," I told Duncan, in the same tone of voice I'd used over and over, to reassure him that David was coming too. Afraid to venture outside, I held class in the cave. I was scratching the final word in the ground when Andrew appeared in the chamber.

"He came back, like you said, Mommy!" Duncan squealed in delight. Andrew said nothing. He dropped his knapsack and sat down cross-legged in front of the last word.

twenty-one

The worst was over.

The trembling and the terrible thirst. The sweating and the dreams that made no sense, that went on and on, shooting out bright, astonishing colors and then pure alabaster.

Now he lay quietly in the silence of the cave, candles lit around the chamber, illuminating stories he had made himself. The lion who played chess and the serpent who served as the pet of a king. So many times over the past five years, he had awakened to face the absence of his own stories. He had lived and formed their center, and yet he could not recall them. He wanted to know but didn't want to know, and even if he asked, other people would not tell them. They kept to themselves the ridiculous things he said or the way he missed the toilet when he pissed, they held his stories hostage in some mistaken belief that this would force a change. But part of a drunk's punishment was having to combat silence with a brand of his own, and make up for the missing stories with a thousand wordless gestures.

He moved his legs a little, sighed. The woman whispered to her son before coming over to lay a cloth on his head, one soaked in the lake of blind fish. Her hand was light on his forehead; the boy's face was serious.

"Is he still sick?" the boy asked. His voice was anxious, a whisper, as though he was afraid that any sign of brattiness would bring about a turn for the worse, like exposing a man with pneumonia to the night air.

"Yes, he's still sick, baby."

"I don't want to go to school today, I want to take care of Andrew."

The statement made the detective smile, and the boy and the woman, surprised, smiled back at him. He had betrayed all of them. The woman, the boy, the husband in Ohio who paced his kitchen and stared at the phone. And yet he couldn't ignore the transformation in himself. He had chosen a side, a faith. How could he have ever thought her insane, now that the glaring proof was gone?

The husband would be on the trail by now, realizing something had gone wrong.

The woman and the boy sat beside him. He reached up slowly and touched the boy's face.

"He's better!" the boy cried.

"Andrew," said the woman. "We have been so worried about you."

He had a plan. And once he had convinced her of it, he would tell her everything.

twenty-two

Andrew was not in the cave when I awoke. I found him on the lookout rock, gazing at the river. It was strange to see him standing up after three days of watching him sleep.

His beard had grown back, covering the scar.

"You feel better, I guess," I said.

He nodded but didn't take his eyes from the river.

"I wanted to apologize. I mean, for making you stay with Duncan and me. I didn't know you'd get so sick."

"It wasn't your fault." He sat down on the rock, letting his bare feet dangle. I sat next to him.

"I haven't seen any Rangers," I said. "Maybe those campers didn't turn us in."

He shrugged. "Maybe it's a great story of adventure for them. Or maybe that one guy was so drunk he thinks he dreamed it."

"How long have you—"

"Been a drunk? Quite a while. Got worse and worse. I guess I didn't know how bad it was."

"How do you feel?"

"Strange. Kind of hollow."

"Do you still want a drink?"

"Hell, yes. But I'm not ever going to drink again. I know that now. I know a lot of things. Everything is so clear. Are things clear for you, Martha?"

I knew what he was asking me. I wanted to tell him again that I was married, that we could never be together, but the words wouldn't form.

I hadn't been dreaming long when I opened my eyes to pitch darkness and a curious tension. Back in Ohio, sleeping and waking were carefully separated by the quality of the light that seeped under the window shade. Black meant the dream could continue, gray meant the dream was threatened, and white meant the dream was irretrievable. Here, I had to linger a moment, my dream fading in and out and finally leaving me entirely as I lay with my eyes open, the same darkness that once terrified me now as familiar as wallpaper or carpet or the feel of flannel sheets. My son slept soundly by my side, his breath as subtle and defining as the brush of a cave cricket across my bare arm.

Someone called my name. It floated around the cave, so insubstantial that it might have come from anywhere, a warlock or an angel, beckoning from the frozen center of a half-finished story. But I knew who was calling me, and the tone invited a choice. I wasn't up to the task, but the voice called again and I stood up, leaving the candles unlit, realizing the sound came from a farther chamber, and when it paused, the silence in its wake had a lower density than that of the rest of the cave. I walked toward the voice, hearing underneath it the skittering of cave crickets and the dripping of water. The stones felt smooth and cool beneath my feet, and I surprised myself at how surely I moved in the dark. Through rote I'd picked up the tricks of bats, which can fly through a room stark blind and dodge even fishing line.

I reached the place in the back of the chamber where the corridor opened, then sank to my knees and began to crawl, cautious because I remembered an abutment of limestone that could collide with my head. My breath was even, my eyes wide open. I felt prehistoric, ancient in my movements and my thoughts. They were based on primary need: fire, water, warmth, and words so simple as to be unspoken.

I didn't know what to say as I reached him and he drew me close to him, his skin warm and smooth. I moved my hands down his bare body, feeling the ridge of his spine. I was wearing only a T-shirt and a pair of panties whose lace trim had come unraveled through repeated washings in the river. Andrew removed them both, and I wanted to slow things down or maybe even retreat. I'd told myself that we were going to talk, but not a word had been spoken after my name. I thought I had forever to make my decision, as much time as it takes a calcite bird to grow a beak, or a bowl to form in limestone under the steady drip of water. Time, though, sped up suddenly, like a river that decides it needs to reach the sea by dawn, and we were seized by evolution, our eyes shutting and receding, Andrew's body covering mine, our skin turning pale and translucent, my fingers in the dust, moving back and forth, my wedding band rubbing bright as a star against the dolomite floor.

twenty-three

Morning. At least light that hinted in that direction, as I left the cave and started down the bluff alone, no shoes, already limping in anticipation of stepping on a brier or a sharp stone. I had thought I could leave my crime back in the cave when I entered the desert. The pain in my side proved me dead wrong, and I couldn't bear to look down at the wedding ring on my hand.

I had counted on the act of sex staying self-contained, but even the small ache when Andrew entered me formed a continuum back to David, reminding me of how long it had been since David and I had been together this way. I had thought I could forget my marriage the way I forgot everything else, yet here it was, broken but still surefooted as it followed me down the bluff. When I reached the river I waded into the water, letting my hands trail in it, feeling river mud between my toes.

I was sitting on a rock, my hair dry but my clothes still wet, when Andrew came into view. He waved when he saw me, and climbed down toward the river.

"Hello." He sat down beside me.

"Hi." I looked in his eyes only briefly, then looked away. A breeze came out of nowhere and blew my hair in my face. Andrew tried to comb it back into place with his fingers.

"Don't."

"Don't what?"

"Touch me."

"Why not?"

I didn't answer. I knew I wasn't being fair to him, but I couldn't help it. I had betrayed David in so many ways that I would have to use the circle of stones in our cave to count them all.

Andrew sighed, clearly mystified. He tapped his bare foot on the surface of the water, making concentric circles fly out toward the farther shore. "You feel guilty," he said. "I feel guilty too, a little bit."

"Why should you? You're not married anymore."

"There are other ways to cheat."

I felt three new bug bites on the side of my calf, and I scratched them into a red blotch that looked like the head of a dahlia. I'd thought about my flowers a lot lately. I'd left them to die in the refrigerator of my shop, petals drooping, rosebuds darkening to the color of soot.

"We need to leave here, Martha."

"I told you, we're not going to another cave."

"I don't mean that. I mean, we need to leave this place. It's only a matter of time before your husband finds you."

I looked at him, surprised. "Why are you worried about that all of a sudden?"

He hesitated. "It's not as remote out here as I thought it was. All these boaters. We're always hiding. Someone's going to discover us, sooner or later. David, or someone else." He touched my arm. "We can have a life together, Martha. You and me and Duncan."

"A life where?"

He pointed down the river. "My geologist friend used to talk about a place past Boquillas Canyon where there's an easy way into Mexico."

"You want to go to Mexico?"

"It's the same desert down there. But there are places we can live where years can pass before we see another soul."

"I'm not going."

"Why not?"

"The cave is safe."

"It's not, and you know it. But maybe it's not about the cave. Maybe it's the fact that your husband can find you here. And maybe you want him to find you."

"Don't be silly, Andrew."

"You yourself said that he didn't understand you, and if he finds you he'll put you in the hospital. I would *never* put you in a hospital." He said this with a slight tremor in his voice, and I wanted to kiss the dark skin of his leg and then push him into the water for complicating my life.

. . .

That night I stood in the lake, candlelight tripping on the water and showing the fish a color they would never be able to appreciate. Duncan paddled on the other side of the lake, winding between the calcite trees, occasionally pausing to wave at me.

The water boiled in front of me, and Andrew rose, his hair slick all over his head. He pushed me against the stone embankment, his face very close to mine.

"Don't," I whispered. "Duncan can see us."

He didn't move, just leaned against me. "I love you," he whispered, "and I love Duncan. Let's get out of here, Martha. We'll go somewhere we can all be safe, forever." He moved his hand down my arm, beneath the water to my wrist and then my hand, finding the ring on my finger, sliding it to the second knuckle before I curled my fist.

twenty-four

I awakened before Duncan and Andrew, some internal rooster crowing a hole in my dream, and extracted myself from Andrew's embrace and dressed quickly. I walked barefoot through the cave, holding my arms out for balance, avoiding teeth and wings and scepters. Andrew had told his most ambitious story the night before. It contained every color in the universe, and it continued for hours, so long that the flashlight beam went out and only Andrew's voice remained. It was a beautiful story, full of twists and turns, whose details were lost to me in the pale air that filled the twilight zone, where creatures grow stronger bones, hunt quicker food, and blink.

. . .

He was waiting for me on a fallen cottonwood trunk, his shirtsleeves unbuttoned and pushed up on his arms. I wondered why he hadn't entered the cave. Maybe he had, and then realized he couldn't see a thing. He gazed at me steadily, his face unshaven, his hair a bit longer, grayer at the temples. His eyes were still blue, but they had a cloudy look, and his skin was sunburned into a false health.

The night before, he'd almost stopped existing, when Andrew put his arms around my body and whispered in my ear. I almost gave in to that temptation, that promise of peace. My ring almost slid off my finger and sank to the bottom of the lake.

I couldn't say that I was surprised to see him. This was the land of sudden oddities. Lizards that sounded like birds, rocks that grew rainbows, spiky plants that turned out to be edible in the very center. A little burst of wind pulled his collar up and rumpled his hair. When he straightened his collar I saw that he still wore his wedding ring, and I looked down, afraid that mine was still suspended on my knuckle. When I saw it on the base of my finger I wanted to show it to him as proof that I couldn't forget him.

I had feared this moment for so long, but now, looking at him, I felt a wild and desperate hope that he had turned back into himself. By my left foot were the remains of Duncan's lesson from the day before, cut into the rocky soil and left there for the moon to read. "Journey," and "silence," and "hammer." I hoped he had seen the words, and understood that I was still a good mother. I still cared if our son could read and write. So many words, swept over with a cottonwood branch and then rewritten.

"David," I said.

twenty-five

He stood up, looking at me.

"It's good to see you," I said. "We don't get many visitors dropping by the cave, except for the occasional Jehovah's Witness."

He didn't smile. Instead he looked over at the opening of the cave. "I can't believe this," he said in a scratchy voice.

"Believe what?"

He pointed at the cave. "You've been living in there?"

"It's not what you think it is."

"Dark and cold?"

"Well, it's that. But it's more than that. You'll see." I wasn't sure about the protocol between a man and the wife who abandoned him. Should I embrace him? Shake his hand? I would have loved to touch him, unbutton his shirt and run my hands down his thin body to ensure that I wasn't still dreaming. But that gesture seemed unbearably rude.

"How did you find me?"

"I looked through all your papers. Got your phone records. Talked to every friend you ever met. Even got up one night and walked around the house, the path you used to take when you couldn't sleep. I tried to imagine what you'd been thinking. I even went to that shrink, but he had no answers for me. I hired a private detective, but he disappeared too. So I started again, on my own. Went back and talked to all the neighbors again. Read your old letters. Went through all your old invoices at the flower shop . . ."

"How were the flowers?" I asked, realizing too late the absurdity of my question.

He stopped for a moment. "There was one rose still alive," he said, "in the corner of the refrigerator. Its bud hadn't opened. I took it home and it bloomed on our breakfast table."

His voice was gentler than I remembered, and I felt a sudden gratitude that he would tell me about the one living thing in that shop rather than all the dead ones.

He reached into his pocket and brought something out in his fist. "Here." He opened his hand so that I could see the dried petals.

"Oh!" I said. A gust of wind came up and took them out of his hand, scattering them around the rocks.

"Sorry." He watched them fly away.

"No, David. Thank you. That means a lot to me."

He put his hands in his pockets. "When I went through your invoices, I was looking for repeat customers. Friends or associates you had that I didn't know about. There were a lot of them.

I talked to more housewives than I could count, and one man with seven mistresses."

"How were you getting your work done, David?"

He looked bewildered. "I wasn't working. How could I work?" He lowered his eyes. A dragonfly materialized from nowhere, and hovered near the stubble of his cheek.

"You lost your job?"

"I quit."

I thought of all the pictures that used to line his office walls, of David making his deals and scouting his locations. Now the pictures had been replaced, and the new ones showed David meeting with the private detective, making phone calls to Texas, opening the creaky door of a dark flower shop, sitting alone at the breakfast table, a single rose blooming.

"I'm sorry," I said.

"One of your customers, name of Ed Godwin, came in every week, according to the invoices. He was a strange old coot, had a house full of newspapers and a vase full of dead carnations on the table. At first he said he didn't know anything. Instead he told me about his wives, how beautifully they'd danced, how he'd loved them so equally he couldn't to this day pick one over the other. And he told me how they both died in his arms, one in 1948, from kidney failure, and the other in 1967, from cancer." David had remembered these facts with precision; I used to read his drilling reports and see the same love of detail. "He said he had no idea where you went, but I had a sense that he was lying.

"So I started visiting him every few days. I let him keep talking. He knew where you were. I knew it. And one day I said to that old man, 'You know my wife. You've seen how beautiful she is. At least as beautiful as your wives. She liked to dance too.

Just like your wives. She's sick. She's sick and she's run off in the middle of the night. If you know where she is and you don't tell me, you're responsible for what happens to her. You say two wives died in your arms. What if my wife dies out there, away from my arms? All alone? Is that what you would wish on another man?'"

I could picture the two of them in the old man's kitchen, bentwood chairs, curtains with patterns of iron-cross begonias, linoleum curling around the baseboards. The old man never had a chance with David, who could find petroleum in bedrock, and the gooey vulnerability in an old man's bones.

"What do I look like?" I asked David.

He searched my face. "You're tan. Your hair's a lot shorter."

"They're putting in a Supercuts next fall, in a cave down the river."

It was clear that the absence of my humor had not contributed to his grief. Now that the light had sharpened, I could see dark circles under his eyes, stains on his shirt, little purple berries caught in the cuffs of his pants. He flicked a centipede off his arm.

"You haven't even asked about Duncan."

"I'm afraid to ask."

"He's fine. He's happy."

He absorbed this information, started to say something, and changed his mind. "I've thought about him every second of every day," he said at last, "when I wasn't thinking about you. I can't stand it, how much I miss him."

"He misses you too."

He said nothing. What could he say, to the woman who had stolen his son from him in the middle of the night?

The centipede was crawling on his shoe. He shook it off.

"He's happy here, David. I know you don't believe me, but it's true. He can name most of the flowers around you, and he can spell just about anything. Look." I pointed at a word written in the ground. "We have lessons."

He closed his eyes. "Be quiet, Martha. Just don't say any more."

I withdrew my pointed toes. "I know you think I'm crazy, dragging Duncan out here. But I had my reasons. And it's worked. He loves the cave and he loves the river and he—" *Loves Andrew.*

"Let's talk about it later," David said in a tired voice.

"You haven't slept, have you?"

"Not at all, the last two days." He opened his eyes. "Why did you choose this place, out of everywhere in the world? It's not safe out here. The rangers told me there were flash floods, and mountain lions."

"No janitors, though."

His eyes narrowed. "Rattlesnakes," he said. "Scorpions."

"Well, you have to know what you're doing." I said the words hard, but I didn't mean them that way. I meant only to make a case for myself, my own capability. At the same time I'd been trying to judge the sound of my voice the last few minutes. Was it the voice I had before Linda died, or after?

"Are you coming back with me?" he asked. It was a plaintive question, and I felt his pain so clearly, I saw the kitchen, and the stains on the bottoms of the cups he'd washed. I saw the wall clock. I saw the answering machine blinking and him leaning into it as he punched the button. "You didn't have to leave," he said. "We could have worked it out. We can still work it out. I'm your *husband.*"

"You didn't understand. I'm not saying it's your fault. Maybe you couldn't help yourself. But I couldn't be there anymore and know your point of view."

"I'm not angry with you. Not at all. I just want to take care of you. I promise, I'll make you better, if you'll just give me a chance."

"Make me better? How about you?"

"I don't want to argue. I'm just so tired."

I moved closer to him and put my hand on the side of his face, pressure that let the air out of his lungs. "I know you can't believe this, but I've thought about you every second of the day. Even when I didn't know I was thinking of you, you were there. A subtext for everything, even blinking."

He reached up and held my wrist.

"Are you all right, Martha?"

The sound of his voice, so soft and full of concern, broke my heart. I imagined him out there on a raft, hitting boulders and spinning around in the water. Oil, not water, was his element. He'd done all this for me.

My guidebook had no advice about what to do when a husband enters the cave of a cheating wife and finds her lover inside. I'd never worried about David being unfaithful to me. He wasn't that kind of man. And even a week before, I never would have thought I'd be unfaithful to him. We walked through the twilight zone together, and then the shadows fell over us. A few more steps and we were in total darkness, and I wondered whether I'd been dreaming all this, whether in reality it was three in the morning and there were no birds calling outside, no sun rising, no estranged husband walking beside me. David put a hand on my shoulder to steady himself.

"Duck here," I said.

"Why?"

"There's a stalactite right in front of us. Looks like a bowie knife."

"How can you walk like this in the dark?"

"I can feel it."

I couldn't tell whether he was frightened or curious. I squeezed his hand. "Stop for a minute, David."

"What is it?"

"There's someone else in this cave. Besides Duncan."

He dropped my hand. "Who?"

"A friend. I just wanted you to know."

There was no response in the darkness.

"David?" I put my hand out and touched his arm.

"Who is this friend?" He sounded suspicious. Like all blind cave creatures, he'd picked up on my tone of voice.

"Never mind. You'll see in a minute." I took his hand again and pulled him along, turning the final corner and walking into the chamber.

Andrew crouched in front of the stone oven with his back to us. Candlelight played on the bare skin of his shoulders.

Duncan was nowhere in sight.

"Where's Duncan?" I asked.

"I think he went into the other room," Andrew replied, still turned to the stove.

"Who are you?" David demanded. Andrew froze at the sound of his voice, stood up and turned around.

The two men stared at each other.

"David," I said, "this is Andrew."

"His name isn't Andrew," David said. "It's William. William Travis."

"What are you talking about?"

"Tell her," David said.

"It's not what you think, Martha. He hired me to find you. But—"

"David hired you?"

"He's not the greatest detective, though," David added, his voice tight. "Usually you don't have to worry about the detective disappearing too."

"I don't believe it." My mind was racing in crazy circles. "You two were working together? Against me?"

"It's different now!" Andrew insisted. "I love you!"

"You love her? She's my wife!" David charged up to Andrew and gave him a push. "Did you sleep with her? Did you take advantage of a sick woman? I'll put you in jail for that."

"Get your hands off me," Andrew warned, and the cave filled up with the threat of war.

"Duncan!" I shouted. "You stay where you are. Don't come in here."

"Martha's not sick," Andrew said. "She's fine. Maybe you're sick."

"You're a fine one to make that diagnosis! After I found out all about you! How you're a pathetic drunk who got thrown off the police force! And you couldn't keep your own wife, could you?"

"David," I said, "stop trying to . . ." My words trailed off. Duncan had appeared in the room.

"There he is, David," I said, pride in my voice. "There's your son." I pointed to the back of the cave.

"Duncan?" David took a few steps and stopped. His shoulders slumped, and he sank to the ground and put his head in his hands. Bewildered, I knelt down next to him, close enough to hear his shallow breathing. I had never seen him cry, not at his wedding, or the birth of his son, or the funeral of his father.

Duncan stood in the candlelight, watching.

I put my hand on David's shoulder.

"Daddy?" said Duncan. He moved closer, turning his head sideways to get a better look at his father. "Daddy, I knew you'd find us. I knew it all along."

twenty-six

David's head was still buried in his arms. I stood there, absolutely mystified by the turn of events, wanting desperately to blow out all the candles, dive back into my sleeping bag and hope the sun went back to its own sleeping bag. Starting the day over seemed like a fine idea.

"Tell him to leave," Andrew said.

"Mommy," Duncan protested, "I want Daddy to stay."

"Daddy doesn't have to go anywhere, Duncan. And Andrew, or whatever your name is, you shut up. Just go outside."

"Daddy!" Duncan tapped at his father's shoulder.

"Leave Daddy alone for a few minutes, honey. Go outside."

Andrew looked at David. "Whatever he says, don't trust him, Martha."

"That's a pretty funny thing to say," I answered, "coming from you."

Andrew motioned to Duncan and they glided away into darkness, leaving the two of us alone. I sat down next to my husband, watching him. I'd done this to him. I'd taken the most stoic man on earth and shattered him. A grainy picture of me hung from the wall of every master bedroom in the world, a warning to couples who think they know each other.

"I'm sorry, David," I said, and I truly was. I had tried so hard to keep him from my thoughts, but the desert that offered amnesia for every other memory wouldn't give me this last gift. I wasn't sure he would have been able to find me had I truly forgotten him. Now he was here to take us back. He'd probably already paid for our hotel room in Alpine, and our flight back north.

His hands had fallen away from his face, his head was turned to the side, and his breathing was deep and slow. I touched his shoulder. "David?" He was fast asleep, exhausted from his days on the river and all the weeks before that. I sat and watched him for an hour or two, my legs crossed and my hands folded in my lap. I found my CD player and tried to turn on a John Denver song, but no sound came out. The batteries were dead. Absence of music, presence of husband. A cave that felt suddenly cold. I took Andrew's tin cup and filled it with the clear water from the lake, drinking it slowly, then found a blanket and draped it over David's shoulders. He didn't even move.

When I reached the river, I saw Duncan first, standing knee-deep in the water. Andrew was sitting on the rock beyond him, his knees drawn up and his hand on his chin. It seemed like an era had passed since we had made love. I supposed this was guilt padding itself with time, the same way a child stuffs Kleenex down his pants before a spanking.

"Hi, baby," I said, approaching Duncan.

He backed out of the water and sat on the bank. "Is Daddy still crying?"

"No. He's asleep."

Duncan looked as if he'd been crying too. "What's wrong with him? Isn't he glad to see me? He didn't even talk to me."

"Of course he's glad, honey. It's just that he's very tired from trying to find us, and he needs to rest. He'll talk to you later."

"I want to show him the cave. The other rooms and the stories and stuff."

"You can show him. He'll like that."

I glanced at Andrew, who caught my eye and quickly looked away.

"Daddy's sad," Duncan informed me.

"Yes. But he'll be better, as soon as he sees that you're all right and you're happy. You are happy, aren't you?"

He nodded.

"You don't blame Mommy for taking you out here?"

He shook his head, and I kissed his cool face and walked down the river to Andrew's rock. He had left a space for me next to him. We'd watched the sunsets from that rock together, the colors in the sky different every night, but red always the dominant one. Once, yellow had strayed into its path and everything turned orange before it was over. I sat down and together we watched the water run by. I could tell that Andrew had a lot to say, and that if he scratched his words on the ground they would fill the desert, stretching from cactus to cactus, disappearing in the cane and coming out the other side, decorating the riverbed, even filigreeing themselves on the empty mud nests of swallows.

"So how's everything, Detective Who Once Went by the Name of Andrew?"

"It's Will," he said. "Will Travis. But I still prefer 'Andrew.'"

"Nice to meet you." My voice was cold as ice. "You were pretending all along to be someone else. How many lies did you tell me?"

"I didn't lie to you. My wife really did leave me. I really did get stabbed in a bar. I really was a drunk. I really needed to forget everything."

"It doesn't matter how many truths you told. *You* were a lie."

"I lied at first. But then, I promise, I wasn't lying anymore. I believed in the things you believed in."

"Who knows whether that's true or not?"

"No! Will you listen to me?" His voice was urgent. "Will you listen for Duncan? Because I'm going to tell you this before you get hurt. Your husband doesn't love Duncan."

He was deliberately trying to antagonize me now. "You're crazy. He's Duncan's father!"

"Yes, yes, but I love Duncan more. You'll see that, Martha."

"Fine. Nice talking to you." I started to slide off the rock. He caught my wrist, pulled me back. "What does he mean to you?"

"He's my husband."

Andrew looked at me pleadingly. "I love you."

"He loves me too." I was trapped between two competing kinds of love, a river squeezed by its border countries.

"But I understand you. He never will."

"You know what? David's never lied to me. Not once."

"He's going to try to take you back. You know that. What am I supposed to do if he starts dragging you out of the cave? Just stand there and watch him?"

I glanced behind me. Duncan was lying on his back spread-eagled, staring up at the clouds. "I don't think it will come to that."

"We have choices," Andrew said. "We can get away from him."

When I returned to the cave, David was awake and sitting on the stone embankment at the edge of the lake. He had lit the last of the candles; the flames reflected off the water, and the light showed circles under his eyes so dark they couldn't be real. It had been a long time since the chamber was this bright. I could see the details of the calcite trees, and the thin parts of the formations glowed orange.

The stories in this cave had multiplied and joined one another. All archetypes had been represented, all story lines. They crossed and crisscrossed; witches dated generals, and wolves became captains of ships. Princesses married lions, birds circled deep in the sea. You could even say that the stories had become deranged; patterns didn't exist anymore; justice prevailed, in a sense, but often came at the expense of the innocent. I didn't know when the stories ran away from us. David was here to impose order, to convert imagination into stone.

"When did you wake up?" I asked him.

"A few minutes ago."

"I was down by the river."

He waited a long time to speak, or it seemed like a long time.

"So you've slept with him." It wasn't a question, just a flat statement.

"Yes. And I feel terrible about it." I had betrayed my husband twice. First the flight, and then the lover.

"I'm so sorry. I never thought it would happen. I wasn't even going to let him in the cave. I whittled a spear . . ." I gave up. The explanation sounded insane.

"Don't blame yourself, honey. He took advantage of you. You're not yourself."

"I think I'm more myself than I've ever been."

"I hope not." He peered into the water. "Are those fish?"

"Yes."

"They look funny."

"They're blind."

He cupped a handful of water and let it run off his fingers. I sat down beside him.

"I don't blame you for anything, rationally," he said. "But you don't know what it did to me. Waking up in that empty house. All those days of waiting, not knowing whether you were dead or alive."

"I never thought it would hurt you so much. You were always so strong. I thought you'd—"

He stared at me. "Get over you? Get over Duncan? After you left, there was no one to be strong for. No one needed me for anything." His hand moved into the water, breaking the surface. "You can see everything here," he said idly. "You can see straight to the bottom."

"We swim in here. I like to sink down underwater and open my eyes."

He looked around the chamber. "You're living in a fairy tale."

"What's wrong with that?"

"It's not real."

"Who's to say what's real?" I slapped at the surface of the lake and the fish took cover in the calcite forest. "You were never proud of me, David. At least, you never said you were. You were the smart one, the successful one. Aren't you at all impressed that I made this work, that I kept your son safe, that he's happy and playful and smart? Can't I have credit for anything?"

"Oh, Martha," he said, his voice sad and sweet. "When you say that, it breaks my heart."

It had been so long since he'd mentioned his heart or how fragile it might be. I wanted to put my hand on his chest, feel the beat of this organ he'd just begun to notice.

"Do you love him, Martha?"

The urgency in his voice made me take his hand. He didn't pull it away. So many nights I'd wished him vulnerable like this, under the bedrock and into the ooze of intentions and hopes. I'd wanted him to be romantic in this desperate way. But I couldn't will away the story of Andrew. And even as my fingers slid in between my husband's, tightening, I wondered what Andrew was doing, I wondered about his thoughts and his fears. I had left him without telling him what I was going to do, and I wondered which way his body was posed in the absence of an answer.

"I think I love him," I said.

David's fingers straightened and fell away.

"And me?" he whispered. "Do you love me?"

"I love you more, David. More than Andrew, more than any other man. It's not convenient for me to feel that. But it's true."

"Then come back with me. I'll make you well. I'll make you happy. I promise I will." I could see his tears, yet I remembered Andrew's warning. *Your husband doesn't love Duncan.*

The candles were burning low. In a matter of hours we would have no more; they would turn extinct in a world that needed them. My voice was a whisper. "I'll make Andrew leave. This can be your home as well. We'll live here together and we'll be so happy, David, I promise you we will. You'd be surprised what you can forget here. You just have to believe. Can you believe, David? Sometimes I even forget that Linda is dead."

My words made him scramble to his feet. "Oh, God," he said. "Oh, God!" Another candle died. "Don't you think I want to believe? Don't you think that would make me happy? You're so convincing. It kills me how convincing you are. This morning I thought I saw him in the candlelight. Just for a second I thought he was real."

I looked at him, bewildered. His words made no sense at all to me. He started crying again and I wanted to go to him, put my arms around him and tell him that everything would be all right, if he only had faith. But he had no faith, and to prove it he said, one more time, what he had first said back in Ohio.

"Martha, Linda is alive! She wasn't killed in that blast. Duncan was killed. Our son is dead."

twenty-seven

My husband was crazy. Completely insane. I was screaming at him at the top of my lungs, so loud that Andrew, who must have been listening at the entrance of the cave, came bursting into the chamber of light.

"What's the matter? What's the matter?" he demanded.

"He's crazy!" I pointed at my husband accusingly, my feet moving, kicking over a candle. "You shut up, David! Shut up!"

"It's true!" David shouted. "I can't pretend!" He whirled around to face Andrew. "You tell her it's true, Will!"

"Tell her what?"

"Don't say it!" I shrieked, but David said it again, anyway.

Andrew took a breath. The cave fell silent, and we waited for him to pass judgment on one of us. "He's not dead," Andrew said finally.

David took a step toward him. "You lying bastard. Do you think you're helping my wife by agreeing with her? Do you think she'll ever get better this way?"

"She is better," Andrew said calmly. "She's happy. Don't you want her to be happy?"

"Of course I do. I'm her husband. But this is a lie!"

Duncan had appeared in the chamber and was standing quietly in the dim light, watching us.

"Is Duncan here right now?" David asked.

"Yes," I said.

Duncan's eyes widened when I pointed to him.

David looked at Andrew. "And you see him too?"

"I didn't at first. But I do now." Andrew looked at me. "I swear to God I see him, Martha."

"Honey," David pleaded, "I can take care of you. I can make you well. We can start over. We can have another child."

I felt calm. "I don't need another child, David. I *have* a child."

"Where did you say he was, Martha?" David's voice had a strange tone in it, and I regretted leaving my medication to the wind. My husband needed it now.

"He's standing right there." I pointed again. Duncan looked uncertain.

Suddenly David was right in front of Duncan, raising his hand high in the air. David had never struck his son, not so much as a tap. But I realized, with horror, that he was going to try to run his hand through Duncan's chest.

"No!" I screamed.

David's hand came down.

Andrew grabbed his wrist.

David shoved Andrew with his free hand. Andrew shoved him back, into a stalactite, which broke with a loud crack. David fell to the floor but quickly jumped to his feet and lunged at Andrew.

"Stop it!" I shouted, but it was too late. They were punching each other, grappling on the floor of the cave, candles going out as they fought in gradations of shadow. I rushed to Duncan, knelt behind him and covered his eyes. I didn't want him to see what had happened to our dream. Andrew and David cursed each other, rolling on the floor, calcite formations darkening one by one. The formations still visible looked like nothing but stone.

The fight was over, and there was no telling who had won and who had lost. David and Andrew sat on opposite sides of the cave chamber, two candles left burning, one lighting up Andrew's arm and lap, and the other playing on the side of David's face. No one spoke.

Duncan and I sat together in the dark, watching the two men. I felt so sorry about the broken formations; I couldn't face that old man again. It was so unfair, the delicacy of calcite, the centuries that went into the shapes. Now the stories would never be the same.

A candle wick sputtered, and Andrew's arm flashed orange and black, and disappeared. David's eye blinked from across the cave. I heard Andrew stand up and walk toward me and then past me out of the cave. Duncan gently extracted himself from my arms and followed him. I let him go. I knew that Andrew was going down to the river, where my rubber raft was hidden in a stand of cane. He'd checked it a week before, said it was dirty and deflated but free of punctures. He was going to inflate the raft, restore it to its former shape, put it on the river and float away to Mexico.

It felt sad but necessary to watch David's face in the candlelight, and I didn't try not to feel my love for him. I had not cried since the day of the bomb, but I allowed myself now, as cave crickets skittered around, and shadows moved down David's face, and the first healing drop of water ran down the broken stalactite and began the work of rebuilding.

"It's nice to see you, David," I said finally. "I've been watching you in the candlelight. You're so beautiful. You always were."

David picked up the last candle and crawled over to me, holding the light near my chin so that I felt the heat spreading over my face.

"And you, Martha," he said, "are beautiful."

He had a cut on his cheek, and his nose was bloody.

"I'm sorry about Andrew," I told him. "I never meant to be unfaithful to you. But I need him now, don't you see?"

David put the candle down between us and held my face. "We have each other."

"That was enough before Duncan was born. It's not enough now."

"Don't leave me."

"I have to."

"Where are you going?"

"Mexico."

"Oh, Martha." His hands were warm around my face. The candlelight came up between his forearms and washed across his eyes.

"I don't want to leave you, David, when you're sick. But I have no choice. Do you think you'll get better someday?"

"I don't know. I wonder the same thing about you."

"Remember the morning they brought Duncan to me? He was such a pretty baby. And you came in the room and the nurse put him in your arms. You were so excited. I watched you two from my hospital bed. Who would have thought that the same child who brought us together would tear us apart?"

No one could see us down here. Tons of limestone covered our marriage and I didn't have to follow any rules about separation. So I kissed him until the flame between us made my right elbow too hot to continue. I stood, the darkness cooling my face and my mouth, and left the cave.

I was halfway down the side of the bluff when I heard David's footsteps behind me.

Andrew and Duncan stood on the bank. Duncan saw us and waved. Andrew had the raft inflated and sitting in the sparkling water, the rope tied around a tree limb to keep the boat from floating away. A full moon was out, and so were a million stars. The last time the sky was this bright, Duncan and I were watching our station wagon burst into flames.

When I reached the bank I saw that Andrew had blood on his shirt. He didn't say anything. He knew I'd made my choice.

"Are you ready to go, baby?" I asked Duncan.

"Yes."

"We're going someplace new, baby. A beautiful place, son, more beautiful even than our cave. Would you like that?"

"Yes," he said, but he was looking at David, who was still struggling down the bluff. "Daddy's not coming?"

"No, honey. Your father's too sad to come."

"But will he visit?"

"Maybe someday." I told him this because the truth would hurt him too much, and I was his mother. I knew what to say and what not to. Duncan stepped into the water. The raft didn't move when he climbed aboard and crawled to his usual place.

"Martha!" David called.

Andrew held his hand out to me. "Let's go," he said.

I looked back and saw David running toward us. Andrew and I waded into the river and climbed into the raft just as David reached the shore.

"Martha! Martha!" my husband shouted desperately. "Don't go, baby. Please don't go!" He plunged into the water. Andrew cut the line, and the current moved the raft away.

"Go back!" I warned David, but he began to swim, frantic strokes as the raft gained speed, and my love for him overwhelmed me, the river moving us closer toward the canyon, starlight reflecting so brightly off the water that I had to shield my eyes.

"Hurry, Daddy!" Duncan shouted encouragingly.

"It's too late, honey," I said. We went around a bend in the river, and David disappeared.

Maybe I imagined him.